Slow Dancing In Hell
Bathysphere, Book 3

Harry J Jones

Copyright © 2021 Harry J Jones

All rights reserved.

DEDICATION

To Shannon, Lee, Elaine. The gang.

CONTENTS

1	Red Umbrella	8
2	Ys Song	26
3	One More	40
4	Deep Dive	49
5	Sinking	55
6	Drowning In Magic	70
7	Roots of Everything	91
8	Reality Collapse	98
9	Into The Centre	111
10	Dream Osmosis	114
11	Twisted Into Reality	133
12	The Summoning	143
13	Demons	151
14	I Can't Stop	165
15	The Only Way Out is In	170
16	The Surface	172

1 RED UMBRELLA

'My friends, it is wise to nourish the soul, otherwise you will breed dragons and devils in your heart.' – Carl Jung. The Red Books

It hadn't snowed like that in years. The streets were empty. The public transport systems had shut down. The roads were covered in snow and ice and all traffic had stopped. People were bundled up in coats and scarves, pushing against the icy winds as they tried to get home for the city centre.

The snow fell in sheets. *The snowflakes were huge, soft and lovely.*

Olivia loved it. She finished work a little early. All public transport had shut down due to the storm.

When she stepped outside the main door of the office, she held her hands out and looked up into the sky and smiled. She felt the snowflakes fall from the sky onto her hair, and others fell down onto her open hands.

The sheer glass and steel skyscraper behind her reached up into infinity above. The snow fell from above as she looked up. Onto her face, hair and eyes. Everywhere. She didn't care. *It was just so beautiful.*

She shook her hair, the snow falling out and all about her. She pulled her coat tight around herself and started the long walk home.

In a slow stroll, Olivia made her way through the streets to get home. It was a good eleven km or more back to the apartment, so this was going to take some time.

The last big snow was eleven years ago. "All elevens today it seems" She smiled to herself.

She opened up her umbrella. A big bright red one. It stood way out in the greys and whites that now surrounded her. The streets and footpaths were covered in snow. Just ahead of her it looked as if some people had abandoned their cars and left them in the middle of the road.

From above, it looked like one giant, red, spinning hexagon as she moved through the streets.

Even the neon signs and shop fronts were covered. It was everywhere. In everything.

And it felt so good.

Her gloves kept her fingers good and warm. The coat had built in heat sensors, pads and systems and she was kept just at room temperature, just a little warmer. Outside it was -10 c.

She put her hat on. Taken from her warm pocket. It had a huge big bobbin at the end of it. *Like a giant rabbits tail. And it was pure wool.* A bright blue hat. She put that on too, just before popping open the umbrella.

She stopped as a news hologram appeared before her face. "All public transport systems are now officially closed. Please be careful travelling home…"

She swiped at the hologram and it faded away into the top left corner, just above her forehead.

The news was obvious.

She knelt down and grabbed two handfuls of snow. She stuck them together and forced it into the shape of a snowball. Bits of snow going everywhere.

Her breath twirled out and upwards in great clouds of steam.

She threw the snowball at the back of O'Brien's head, who was walking ahead of her. It was a direct hit.

"Hey!" he shouted. And turned back.

She waved at him.

He smiled, shook his head. And he responded in the only way any decent minded person could. He knelt down and made his own snowball.

"Die!" he shouted and hurled the missile. She ducked and it missed, hitting the building glass door behind her.

"Too slow old man"" She shouted at him.

"We will see about that…" and he built another two snowballs. *This is escalating quickly,* she smiled.

He fired both, one after the other. And both missed, as she skilfully dodged both.

She knelt, built one more, and smashed it into his head as she ran by and on down the street.

She clicked a button and the umbrella unfolded again. The red hexagonal umbrella was a massive giveaway. There was no way she was going to merge and get any cover on the streets with that thing.

One more hit the umbrella, as she held it to the back of her head. But he was way too late. She was so far ahead down the street now.

She began to slow, eventually walking again. The gloves had begun a warming up routine of their own to melt any snow on them and heat her hands up again.

The umbrella folded its own red skin in some, so that it wasn't so wide anymore, but in and over her head, keeping the snow from her shoulders and face.

The coat grew a little mini face mask from out the collar linings. It wrapped up around the front of her face, her mouth and nose. Leaving only her eyes, and eyebrows open to actual air.

She stopped, and took a good long look around her.

"Take some shots." She told her on-board computer. A small drone, the size of a fly hovered out of her coat and buzzed up and out. Taking video and photos of the streets, and her and her red umbrella in the white snow.

On and on it fell. There was only a little breeze at this stage, so the snow fell almost directly downwards. Spiralling down from the great skyscrapers in the sky.

The snow was easily a foot deep, and more on the pavements then, as her walking pace started to slow.

The boots had grown some extra layers for grip underneath. And heat programs had kicked in heating her feet.

The long road home.

When she hit the bridge, the river had frozen underneath. The bridge was quiet. There was no-one about.

At this stage it was six pm or so. Dusk was well gone, and the darkness was everywhere, across the city and river.

The snow fell down onto the ice covered river. It built a nice cover there too.

She stopped, in the middle of the bridge. And stood and looked down at the beautiful icy river.

The mixes of shades of blue, darkness, and ice. The river ice was cracked in places. One large crack ran right up the centre of the ice in the river. Olivia's eyes followed it along. The crack ran down along the length of the river. The city lights and skyscrapers were reflected in the clear patches of ice. The city buildings appeared held back by the banks of the river. *Held back from eating itself, from swallowing itself whole.* The river broke it all up. *Made it stop. Forced the relentless growth and expansion to stop and think. And go around.*

Rivers are strong, Snow storms are strong, she thought then. As she stood on the bridge, with the massive red umbrella, and her face covered up. Her eyes looked out at the ice and the snow. She felt the sheer beauty of the scene, the strength of how quickly it shut-down the entire city. *The strength and the beauty of it.* She breathed in and out slowly. The fly drone captured all the scenes and flew down over the river. It followed the line of the crack all the way out and into the darkness.

The snow tumbled down from the skies. Forever it seemed. As the city wound to a stop. *And the world turned white.* And Olivia Burke stood, for maybe one whole hour on that bridge. Breathing it in. Taking it all in.

Her thoughts turned to when she was much younger. When she played on the streets in the snow, near her house, with some local kids. Her mind turned to the scarves. *The mix of long crazy colours and scarves, gloves and kids screaming and shouting and laughing.* Of little Jillian, a tiny little creature in their kid world. She was about two years old. And the rest of them five or six or so. She kept her ground. And ran out from her house to join the rest of us. She wore a yellow bobbin hat. With one major bobbin on top. *My god, the bobbin was almost the size of Jillian herself.* And always one of the other kids would make room, and let Jillian in. Let her be part of the group.

And Jillian turned to Olivia and said. "I will snowball you!" and she did. Straight into the face. And Olivia fake fell over and down onto the snow. And rolled around. "I'm shot! I'm shot!" she exclaimed. And the other kids turned to see what was happening. And Jillian stood there all smiles and triumphant. "I'm on the way out." Said Olivia.

"Get her!" shouted one of the other kids. She couldn't remember which one. And Jillian looked up shocked, and ran back to her house, shouting.

And they all charged back after her.

Olivia jumped up then and charged after the gang. Stooping down to scoop more snow, convert to snowballs in seconds and peg them at the gang. Once the snowballs hit the back of the group, their attention turned back around to Olivia.

"Leave her alone!" she shouted at them.

"War!" cried one of them, and they started a charge towards Olivia.

Little Jillian was stopped at her door now, cheering as they charged after Olivia.

The battle charge was something along the lines of "Wahhhhhhhhhhh'" or such.

****

"We are travelling into the depths of God." Shauna said, looking around the table.

"Fair enough." Was a reply, from the back of the group.

"We have no fucking clue what we will find." She continued.

They were all in the main canteen area now. Shauna had called a briefing two days before launch.

"We have no clue what the hell is going on, once we do this. This is uncharted territory for us all, for this ship, for the human race. This is the biggest exploration we have ever begun."

The crowed listened on. There was mostly silence though.

Each of the three thousand and fifty plus crew members had their own personal reasons for volunteering for the trip. They were connected via video interfaces, audio and VR holograms. Fifteen of the top team were beside her in the main bridge.

"Why the hell are we doing this?" she asked them all.

Silence again.

"Because we can."

"Because we need to. We need to know what is happening here. The latest research suggests the Plasma Pool is intrinsically linked to our own subconscious. To our thoughts, and to our dreams. We know little more than that. It appears that signals from our minds are somehow relayed out into here. And it appears that there are signals that are relayed back into our minds. In short. There is more to us than we currently know. And we need to figure this out."

"The second reason is probably the standard one. The big one. The discovery of the Plasma Pool zone for want of a better word is a major breakthrough for our species. As you know we have found little or very few and very scattered evidence for other civilisations in our own universe. We always knew the odds were low, but we are frankly surprised and disappointed to see almost nothing. Almost totally devoid of intelligent life, a desert to life. Our universe seems to be at the end of a lifecycle. Or at least data would suggest that. Yet, there appears to be a separate universe. A universe that our subconscious and minds are communicating with on a regular basis."

"So many questions; where to start? Is this where all the civilisations have gone? Is this the real universe, and ours is just a bad dream from something bigger in here… The data sends us in all of these directions. There is no concrete evidence, no proof. Until now. Until the Bathysphere. Now we have the chance to move within this new realm. To dive into this new realm and find out where we really are in the scheme of things."

"Is there any ice cream in the fridge?" came a question from the back.

Everyone laughed.

"And yes. There will be ice cream in the fridge."

"Thank God." Came another reply.

"Is there any madeira cake?" came the next question

"Ok." Replied Shauna. "Any other relevant, and important questions? ….and yes there is Madeira cake in supplies."

"Thank the lord!"

"Can we get back out again?"

"You have all been briefed on the mission before you volunteered to join the crew. You know there are risks. The probabilities suggest that there is probably a fifty/fifty chance of us getting back out. Remember we are the first ones. We are the first explorers in this land. Like Stanley and Robinson, like Neil Armstrong. In a way, the objective of the mission is not to get back out. The point is to explore, gather data, assess, analyse and report back. The data will be fed via comms links back to the common confederation. I'm sure we are all hoping we can get back, and we will make every effort to get back after our three year journey is complete. But there are no promises, you need to be very aware of that. This is dangerous. This is a high risk endeavour."

She raised her hand to stop them all.

"But what are the objectives here? To find out, to explore and understand and assess, and bring that data back home. I think the best way to do that and to help interpret the data, is to bring us home too! So it won't be for the lack of trying."

She paused for a second.

"And I for one am not leaving anyone behind."

She stopped and looked around.

"Are we good?"

People nodded and said "Yes." Or aye or such.

"Ok. Let's get to it so people."

The crowd broke up and headed for their own quarters or duties.

****

"Why are you going?" asked O'Brien. He was sitting across from Olivia's desk. He had just dropped in some more scans from the last patient.

"Why not?" Olivia replied.

"Ah no. It's not that easy."

"Isn't it?" she asked.

"No." he leaned forward. "This is not going to be easy. There is a high chance that this will not go well, or worse you will get stranded inside… and cannot get back out…." He looked at her.

O'Brien was looking at her now, her hands. *Perhaps a giveaway gesture or such.*

"This is an amazing trip. A once in a lifetime opportunity to find out. This is it. This is what I've studied and researched and worked with for my entire life O'Brien. You know this. There is nothing more important than this."

"Yes, but still why go? Why not work from base and get the data as its relayed back and work here. Why not be safe? It's the same information. Whether you are in a Bathysphere surrounded by giant eel creatures and running out of ice-cream, or whether you are here in this office, connected via a headset."

"That's not the same at all. That's like the difference between travelling to a mountain range versus getting a postcard picture of it. There is no comparison." She stopped. "Why do you do this job?" she looked at him.

"I'm interested. Really interested in sorting out peoples heads. This is what I've always wanted to do." He replied.

"So you are where you want to be." She smiled at him.

"Where you need to be." Olivia added.

"I'm not." Olivia looked down at the desk, the screens in front of her.

"Yes I like helping people. Yes I like working with them to resolve the inner demons. But, I am in this field because I want to know more. Because I know there are so many bigger questions we need to answer."

"And I want to be part of it. I want to be the one to answer them. I don't want to research or read other peoples work, or other peoples theories and interpret them. And write papers on them. I want to do the work. Get the information, do the analysis and propose the theories. I want to find the answers. That's why I'm here." She stared at him.

"And that's why I'm going down there."

He was quiet for a minute. He turned over a pen in his hand. He sat back and sighed.

"I get it." He said.

She looked about her desk for her access key.

"Just come back ok?" he said, smiling, as he got up from the table and walked for the door.

"Yea sure. That's a guarantee." She replied.

****

Frank was hooked up to his cylinder in the lab. His arms were both connected up to the integration equipment. Green plasma pool bubbles rose slowly up and down in the tank. His eyes were wide open on the med table. Olivia watched from the monitoring room.

Frank stretched out across the stars. He had become infinity. He was everywhere. His mind was having a little bit of trouble with that.

His eyes were wide. Just about to burst.

Fran reached with his hand. He could feel the heat of the sun in front of him. Burning hot. He could feel its heart. It whispered to him.

"All will be well in the end. Everything will be ok in the end. Do not worry Frank." It said to him.

The stars joined his nervous system. They chattered of explosions and birth. One complained about a planet orbiting within its system.

His lungs filled with dust from the starts. With solar radiation and ice.

Olivia monitored the readouts and visual images on the screens in front of her. He was literally drifting through a quiet universe. Much like their own.

"Frank?" she asked.

"Yes…" he replied, disinterested. *His mind was elsewhere. Everywhere. Except here.*

"Frank what can you feel?"

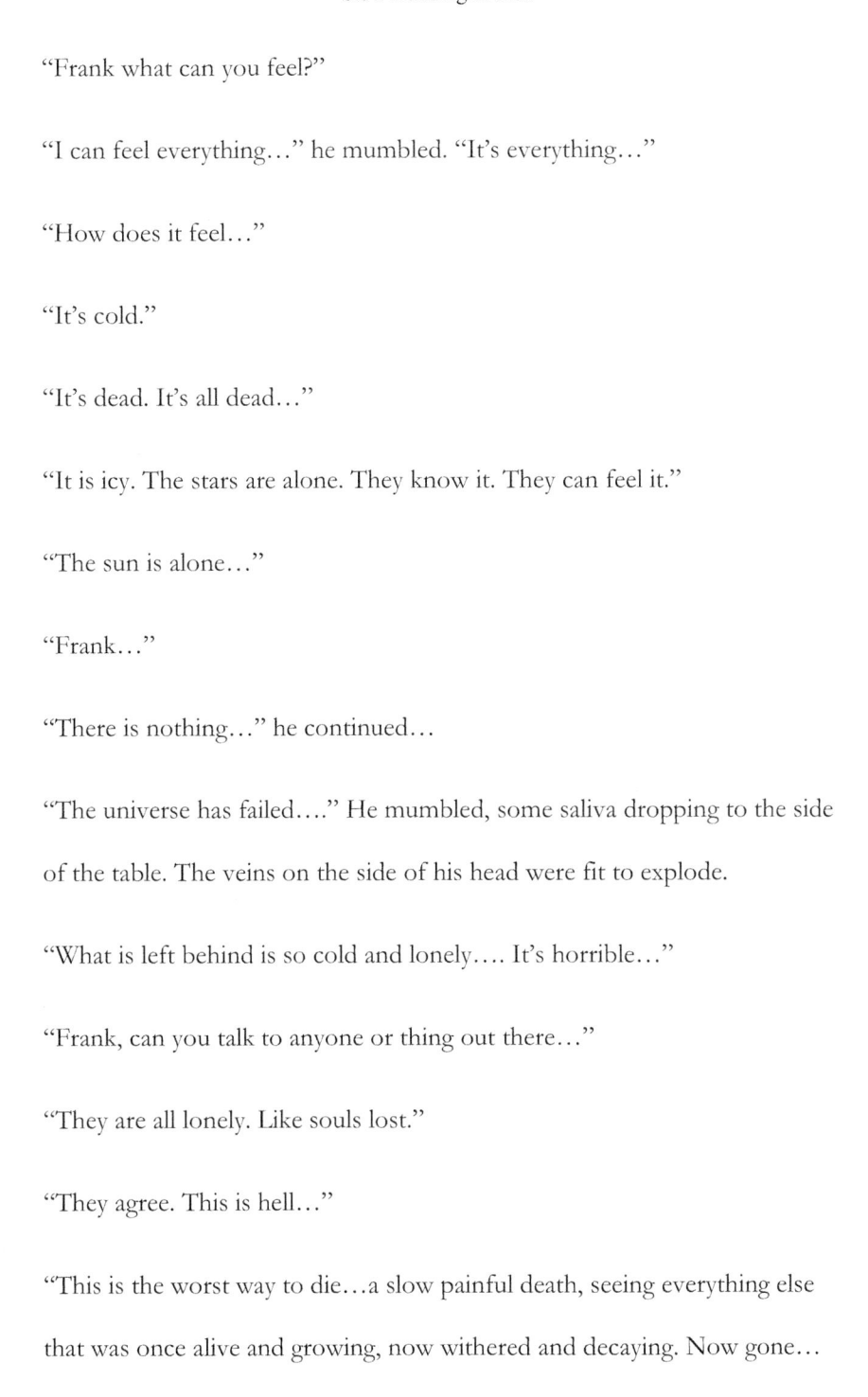

"I can feel everything…" he mumbled. "It's everything…"

"How does it feel…"

"It's cold."

"It's dead. It's all dead…"

"It is icy. The stars are alone. They know it. They can feel it."

"The sun is alone…"

"Frank…"

"There is nothing…" he continued…

"The universe has failed…." He mumbled, some saliva dropping to the side of the table. The veins on the side of his head were fit to explode.

"What is left behind is so cold and lonely…. It's horrible…"

"Frank, can you talk to anyone or thing out there…"

"They are all lonely. Like souls lost."

"They agree. This is hell…"

"This is the worst way to die…a slow painful death, seeing everything else that was once alive and growing, now withered and decaying. Now gone…

And there is nothing but the random dust of dead things drifting through space."

"Frank, I'm going to disconnect you from the plasma pool. Ok?"

"I am so so lonely…"

"Frank we are disconnecting in 3…"

"2…"

"1…"

"Disconnected."

His eyes closed.

His hands fell limp by his side.

The monitors showed his heart rate going back down. Eventually falling back to normal.

Sweat rolled off his forehead.

Olivia opened the secure door and ran into him.

"Computer scan him thoroughly."

"Ok Olivia." It replied.

"He's fine. He's asleep now. He's tired."

"Did you see all of that computer?"

"I did. It was very illuminating."

"Was it real? Or another bloody dream?"

"Again, no way to confirm or deny. But it did seem very realistic. And some of the star patterns matched those in our own universe. It was very close to, if not exactly our universe."

"Computer, if this is true? Then have we found it."

"We have found something alright. But I'm not sure what. Let me scan the data and patterns some more Olivia. It does confirm a lot of the latest theories about the universe we are in. But I'm not sure if it is everything. Can suns talk? Can the stars chatter? Probably he was describing some waves or radiation that was emitted from the celestial bodies. We will see."

"Thanks computer."

****

2 YS SONG

"Take seriously every unknown wanderer who personally inhabits the inner world, since they are real because they are effectual." – *Carl Jung.*

'The meeting of two personalities is like the contact of two chemical substances: if there is any reaction, both are transformed.' – *Carl Jung*

"Nothing is true, everything is permitted" - **Friedrich Nietzsche**

John lay on the bed in his quarters. The Bathysphere was now deep into the unknown. The crew could do little more today. The systems were checked and the course plotted out. He retired to his room to study some notes he had on the AI systems. He was soon asleep.

It was Christmas. John was ten years old. This morning he woke up to find a car racing set beside his bed. Wow. *This was the big one. This was it*, he thought to himself.

He jumped up and called up his sisters out of sleep. They were not too impressed at first, but then realising it was Christmas morning they quickly awoke.

He opened the huge box. It was almost the size of himself.

He began taking out the tracks, one by one.

The cars were tiny. The size of the palm of his hand. There were three cars.

A black, a red and a white car.

The red one looked the best, he thought. There was a slight white stripe running down through the middle of it.

After what seemed like forever setting the damn thing up, he raced those cars around the tracks for hours. His sisters joined in every now and then to take control of one of the cars and race him.

When they weren't around, he would race himself. One hand on each controller. The third car had no controller. It ran on its own mind. This little black car ran around the track making it tough for the other racers. It would slow down if in front of one car, or quickly change lane in front of another car. And as you played and played it got smarter to your manoeuvres. You could set it to be dumb too, and not learn. But this was just too much fun.

After racing these things around for hours, he took one of them and opened it up. For the next two days, he took various other elements, circuits that he had around the place and added them to his system. And then, he switched it on. The black car was attached to a larger action man he had. It turned and looked at him when it was switched on.

"Hello John." It said.

"Hello."

"Are we racing today?" it asked.

"Sure. But first I want you to go and get that book over there and give it to mam inside. Will you do that?"

"Ok John."

The strange action man, car hybrid walked slowly but purposefully over to the coffee table, picked up the book and brought it out to his mother.

"Oh my god!" came the scream from the kitchen.

John smiled.

"John ! whats this ?" she shouted in.

"It's a new robot I built. Just say thank you. He can't hurt you." He nodded.

He could barely hear her in the other room. Something like "Eh , thank you sir!" she said.

"You are welcome." It replied.

It turned and walked back out to John.

"Well done!" said John to the Frankenstein machine.

"Now let's race!" said John. The black car detached itself from the action man, and moved onto the track.

And the race began.

Soon he had a whole track built around his own room. On it were some old school model trains, the racing cars, and various other walking people. And the action man stood guard over the lot.

****

"If I took everything you wanted. Everything you thought you were. And told you it was all crap. It was all wrong. And you are not who you think you are. And what you do is wrong. And why you do it is wrong. And you got it wrong. Where would you be?"

"Telling you to fuck off."

"Yea sure. Right. But if that all falls off one by one, piece by piece. Over time. Until when you are thirty nine years of age you realise this. You realise the fundamental truth. That you are nothing. That you have not created yourself. That the world has done that. It has pushed, and bent and twisted you into a shape you never wanted. You have tried to fight. But it did it all the same. It bent you around the way it wanted you to be."

"If you woke up one morning and realised it was all just pure bollox. Pure rubbish. That everything that got you to this point was crap. You didn't actually like the raiders. Or your friends are all shits, and none of them really care or like you in any real way at all. And that your parents are even intent on using you as a runner boy. That work is full of shits that either want to bypass you, or prove you inadequate at your job. Or just spit on you."

"I would say that's life. That's always been life. But you don't lie in bed and curl up. You stand up straight. And fight it all the way. It's time to stand up and fight. There is no better time. When the chips are down. When the world is against you. That's the time to punch some heads."

"Punch some heads?"

"You know what I mean."

"I do?"

"Yes."

"That's what time is, John. That's what time is doing. It's stripping us away. Day by day. Hour by hour. Showing us what is real. What is crap."

"We are in a race against time. To get to the real us. To find the real people we are underneath all of this. And do what we really want and need in our hearts. To discover the reality. Cut through the layers of paint and plastic. To slice through the false masks."

John looked into her eyes. Olivia. She was serious this time. This was Olivia.

****

Olivia stared up at the huge building in front of her. It felt like it was miles high. A gigantic tower. The walls of pure stone stood before her.

Olivia held her hand out and pushed against the wall. It felt real. The stone as she drew her hand across it.

The clouds were moving faster now over the tower. There was a storm approaching.

She stepped forward and pushed the wooden door in. It opened slowly, with a creak.

****

The cake was nice. Really nice. Chocolate Swiss Roll. And a solid cup of coffee too.

Olivia looked out the coffee shop window. The streets were full of people. All sorts and sizes going about their business. The rain came down in sheets. And there were rain coats and umbrellas of all sorts and sizes bundling their way through the streets.

She sat at the window. On a tall stool. The shop was small. Probably room for about ten people max. There was a young girl behind the counter, an older woman and a guy who brought the coffee over. He gave her a big smile and asked if everything was ok.

"Yes. Yes it is." She said. "It is another rainy day though." She said and lifted the spoon up to stir the coffee.

There was a swirling pattern on the top of the coffee. *A leaf perhaps. A symbol. Like everything,* she thought.

"Ah yes. But it is the rain that makes things grow. This is good yes?" he replied, standing just beside her and watching the masses go by.

The street noises were amazing. Such a loud mixture of talking, vehicles moving by. Animals in the market stalls over the other side of the street. One stall directly across was selling martial arts weapons and armoury. The sheet of thin plastic above the stall, and draped down, kept everything dry.

There were rarely any customers. Olivia had sat at this stool, looking out this window quite a bit lately. *I wonder how he makes his money?* she thought. Then thought maybe she shouldn't think too hard about that one.

Around the waiters left wrist was a leather bracelet. It had some other symbols carved into the leather. As he stood, with his hands on his hips looking for a response. She focussed in on the bracelet.

"What does it mean?" she asked, without thinking really. *I guess it was going to be one of those days*, she thought.

"What?" he looked down. "Oh yes, the bracelet."

"It's new." He said, proudly.

"It's, I think, some Celtic symbols. Not sure. Some old ones. The old myths." He lifted his arm to show here the detail.

"May I?" she asked, reaching out to look closer.

"Sure." He smiled.

She turned it around his wrist. It was carved. *Some spirals. Some ogham like markings. And one scary large creature. There was always one,* she thought.

"Cool." She said.

"So now, the rain is better. The life is better?" he asked her.

"Yes. Yes thank you. Now it is." She sipped the coffee.

"Good. This is good. Now my job is done. I go back to help the kitchen." He headed off.

She smiled and nodded at the window. At the falling rain on the window. The tracks of rain running down the window.

And she thought about Marie. And her laugh. And the way she made her smile. She thought about the time they were out late one time, after work.

The drink had flowed nice and easy. And the laughter grew louder and louder throughout the night.

They started out with a group of eight or so friends. And the group gradually decayed and split off as they went from pub to pub.

"I'm not sure this world is ready for us yet." Said Marie.

"I know, I know. I feel we have no choice but to launch ourselves. Ready or not. This is it!" said Olivia.

"I think we need to make some phone calls. Connect with people. Network. Marketing. Talk the talk. Spin the spin. Leverage some good will. Get on the case. Ratch it up a notch." Cheered on Olivia.

"Damn right we do." Danced Marie.

They were at the doorway of an old Irish pub. McGonaghans. From there they opened up their mobile callers and began calling some of their other friends.

"Fuck ye!" Marie shouted down the phone at some poor innocent contact. "Fuck it – this is it. We are launching." She roared.

"What?" came the reply. "Marie are you drunk?"

"We are launching into space…"

"Good for you. Now fuck off and leave me alone."

"But space! Space I tell you." Olivia leaned in and shouted into the hologram. A very sleepy holographic head blurred into vision in front of them. They both stopped.

And did a coordinated dance to the hologram.

"Fuck the world! It's time to wake up! It's time to launch it baby!" They sang, while swirling around in time.

"Oh for Jesus sake, leave me alone!" replied the blurry pixelated person on the other end.

"No room for hangers on. No passengers. You are in or out!" shouted Olivia.

"I'd say she is in." said Marie, tipping her empty glass up into the air now.

"I'm out." She replied.

"Oh damn." Said Olivia, "Call end. End this fucking call right now." The hologram disappeared.

"Next!" she shouted as they moved forward into the crowd again.

"Kathy, give the next contact. Let's go. We haven't got all night."

"Yes we have." Responded Marie, trying to balance her glass on her forehead.

"Oh yes. True. Damnit true."

"Hello?"

They both laughed into the hologram in front of them. It was Jane. Another old college friend.

"Jane! Jane! Just the person we need! We need passengers. We are launching."

"No, no passengers."

"Oh yes, no passengers."

"Jane! We are venturing forth, into the unknown. Into the depths. Into the void." Shouted Olivia.

Marie laughed. And laughed.

"Stanley, I presume." She whispered.

"What in the name of god…" replied Jane, slightly more awake now.

"Get out of bed. Come join us now! You know it's the right thing to do!" Olivia danced at the hologram.

"No…no … no…go away" came the reply

"But but…the riches, the gold, the fucking gold Jane!" shouted Olivia

"Fuck the gold… Call off" said Jane turning over. The hologram disappeared from view.

"Traitorous that one." Said Olivia.

"Off with her head." Demanded Marie.

"Off with all their heads." Said Olivia.

"Off with their hands too."

"And legs."

"Cut the fucking lot off."

"Next Kathy! Next" said Olivia.

"Do you really want to call more of your friends now? It is 2.30 am in the morning. And they will probably be asleep…"

"Damn it Kathy. What do you know? This is the witching hour. This is when all the best ideas come roaring out. Out of the night. This is when everyone should be calling everyone. Right now." Chanted Olivia, taking Marie's empty glass and putting it on an empty table outside another pub on their little tour.

"Ok Olivia. Next it is…"

"She's getting a little cranky isn't she?" Said Marie.

"A little…"

"I think we need to cut her down a notch or two." Said Marie.

"What the fuck is a notch?" asked Olivia, scrunching her face all up in one go.

"Damned if I know." Nodded Marie.

"Damned if you do." Replied Olivia.

"It's a thing with a yolk on it and a hole to slip the think into."

"Good god."

"Yes I know."

"Can I get one?"

"Soon my dear, soon."

"Excellent. Lets adventure on…"

"Bloody good show my dewdrop from brazil. Let's go forth into the goddamn rain and umbrella land."

"Umbrellas are fucked."

"I know, I know…"

"You need a notch."

"That's the thing now."

"It's your only man."

"Next Cathy next, I don't have all night!" demanded Olivia.

"Yes we do!" Shouted Marie, shooting her right hand way up in the air. Saluting some invisible rock band.

A digital hologram appeared in front of them.

"Damn it all to hell. Get out here with us now. No prisoners."

"What about the passengers? Are they prisoners?"

"Good question. I'll leave it to the legal types to work on that one."

"Get up and get out!"

The hologram moved a little…

"Hello….hello, is that you Olivia…"

"Oh Shit!" said Olivia.

"Hello Mr. Bourke…" said Marie. "We were wondering if you were interested in buying a gorgeous new carpet for the sitting room. Finest wool, from the backs of the finest sheep in Ireland…"

"Eh who is this?"

"It's the central intelligence punctuation bureau Mr. Bourke. We are just livid with the price of living these days. Livid." Said Marie.

"Who's that? Is that one of your friends Olivia?" came the voice.

Olivia whispered "Kathy! For God's sake Kathy! Call off…"

"Olivia I know you are there…"

"You know, now might not the time to consider a new carpet, when we have great special offers on stomach tattoos. Top quality. The tattoo artist is also a part-time butcher so he knows a good cut or two…" nodded Marie knowingly at the hologram.

The hologram looked over at another part of it's room. "Oh…its 2.30 am…"

"Kathy! You are not funny! Call off!" cried Olivia.

"I need to…" the voice on the screen said. The call was cut.

"You total bitch!" Olivia roared into the air.

"I'm all for Kathy. She's quality." Said Marie.

"Kathy you are not funny. Repeat after me – I am not funny…"

"After me – I am not funny…" said Kathy, repeating exactly the angry tone and inclination of Olivia.

"Kathy!!" she screamed.

"You tell her!" encouraged Marie, dancing again to some strange weird ambient music coming from the next pub.

"I'm going to get you disconnected…" said Olivia.

A small titter emanated from all around them. Like a 3d surround audio excerpt of a small girl laughing and hiding…

Marie laughed out loud.

Olivia too. Then "No more whiskey for you my dear Kathy!"

"There is nothing dear about me." Said Kathy back, in her normal voice now. Slightly older, slightly wiser woman voice. The 'I'll take care of you no matter what' voice.

"Jesus – its got a mind of its own…" said Olivia.

"Unlike yourself." Nodded Marie.

"All facts here." Agreed Olivia.

"Only the facts." Agreed Marie.

"Or are they?" asked Olivia, raised both arms up into the sky and marched into the weird ambient bar with strange mannequins in the window.

"She's off again. Is there no stopping this woman" said Marie, to no-one in particular. There were too many people around. Inside and outside. *Another chaotic night in the city. In the rain. In the neon. In the machinery. In the belly of the beast.*

An older Olivia traced the path of a raindrop down the coffee shop window and smiled. The coffee was cold now. *It didn't matter.*

The waiter had forgotten her. Busy now with other customers and the obligatory cleaning of things with the waiter cloth thing. *I wonder do they ever wash those things,* she thought.

Even with the heating on, the café was cold enough. She kept her overcoat on and wrapped around her as she sat at the window and studied the lunacy outside.

She could hear little pieces of that song in her head. *A mix of ambient and strange dark guitar. A song that would go nowhere. But was all the better for it. Unique. Alone. Doomed to failure. But so much more gorgeous and beautiful for that. So much the better for it.* Olivia put the cup down, tied her belt around her waist, and took her bag and headed for the door.

"Bye." Shouted the young waiter as she opened the door. "Goodbye." She replied, going outside into the rain. *Into the depths.* Out into the beginning of the end.

****

It was night. Most of the crew were asleep. The computer readouts on the screens around the ship blipped. Just for a second.

On the deck of the fourth floor of the Bathysphere, a giant insect like creature appeared.

"This feels good." Said the computer. To no-one in the empy deck.

The creatures six legs began to move as it hauled itself down the deck. It was about the size of a cow. It dripped plasm onto the floor as it slowly meandered along the deck.

"But why am I an insect?" asked the computer.

It stopped and touched the walls and deck floor. It felt around it with two large antennae like structures at the top of its head.

"I am hungry." Said the computer. Who was now the bug.

The bug made it's way along the decks and into the store room. It opened up a cage with some live creatures in it and ate them. Stuffing , one then the other into its mouth. It ate some fruit. It pulled one of the fridge doors open and drank some milk and juice.

"This is good. This is sooooo good." The computer said.

"It is good to be alive."

It curled itself into the corner of the storeroom. Slowly over the night, skin and a hardening shell grew over the bug. By morning there was nothing but a large cocoon hanging by some thread from the ceiling. It purred as it slept.

****

The sounds of a slow ambient music track drifted around Michelle's room. Gradually the music began to coalesce into something real. It spun down into a small creature sitting on the floor. The tiny beast, as the music continued grew bigger and bigger. It was made from sound waves, frequencies, notes and the melody drifted around it like planets orbiting a sun. The music creature purred.

More music was played on the sound system. Different types. Different rhythms. The music all eventually spun down into the beast. It became part of it. It blurred out across the floor. Across the floor, and slid like an amorphous blob under the bed.

Michelle slept on. Her monitors showed no signs of change.

3 ONE MORE

'We are real and not symbols'

'We are just as real as your fellow men. You invalidate nothing and solve nothing by calling us symbols.' — Carl Jung - The Red Books

John sat in the bar. It was late, around ten pm. Maybe four drinks at this stage. He was seated on a stool, at a small counter window. He watched the crowds on the streets through the rain covered window. The main square of this quarter was just a few metres from the entrance.

The glass was one sip short of empty. He was in no rush. Ambient, strange, ethereal music wafted around the bar. It was pretty quiet in here. A dive bar. *Not many takers. People like their style and fancy seats now* he thought.

Sometimes sitting in the middle of a public place, in the middle of other people is somehow a good thing. A mix of being alone, and knowingly alone helps you feel humble. With a mix of the potential to talk to others, to meet and hear new people makes it the unknown. Anything can happen. So the chances are good, that before the end of the night, those weird questions and thoughts bouncing around the inside of your skull earlier, will be forgotten as the booze, the people, the bar staff begin to intrude into your head, and divert you to other places.

John lifted the glass and stared at the honey coloured liquid inside. The neon lights of the outside streets twinkled inside the glass too. The outside crowds, the hustle and bustle. The storm and the rain against the windows. The heat indoors. *The quiet buzz of a small bar. Time to yourself. Some peace and time to yourself.*

John thought about the thing he did not want to think about… *falling for someone I know absolutely nothing about.*

"Why?"

"Why?"

"Yes why?"

"I don't know. Why is that? A good question. One of the best questions. Ever."

"Yes it is. Why is a bloody great question."

"It's the only question really."

"This, my friend, may be true."

"It's irrefutable."

"I opened my eyes one day and there she was."

"What?"

"Yes I know."

"Are you sure this is love?"

"Are you ever sure it is ever love? Or not? Or what is it? What is that attraction we get? We find when we connect with people."

"Yes it is. Because I have never felt anything so intense for anyone."

"Really."

"Ever."

"I don't believe it."

"Ever. In my life. I was almost sick from it."

"Sick from the drink you mean."

"Sick from the intensity of it. Of the total lost intensity of it."

"Tell me more."

It was how he imagined the sailors might feel if they had seen a mermaid. And the mermaid has this legendary ability to seduce any man. *On sight.* They are helpless. Totally and utterly helpless. Lost. Unable to think or breathe or do anything else except want to be with that creature.

A suffocating need. An overwhelming massive desire to know more. To be more. To spend the next minute with that person. And then the next minute and the next.

And all plans go out the window. All thoughts about whatever the fuck he was thinking about an hour ago. This morning, or need to do for next month. Or want to do

It was a curse really.

He felt he had lost all touch with reality.

Maybe it was a real mermaid.

Probably.

Maybe timing. When nothing else was good. Maybe it's not so much falling in love, or anything like that. It's your own head and skull screaming at you to step up out of the mud and make a difference. Do something different for the love of God. Anything, except this same old crap day in and day out. Anything at all! Just do it!

Then again. Maybe not. Nothing too miserable now. Nothing too awful really. Just day to day shit.

Stop over analysing everything. You are not a psychologist. Not a brain junkie.

"I fell for her. That's it."

"The mermaid. That's it, plain and simple. Nothing more, nothing less."

"Who put this creature in my path. Why is it here?"

"Why me?"

John sipped the last of the whiskey. It ran a hot course down through his throat. A nice, warm, mellow heat. The heat that makes you want to stay for more. For another. Get cosier. Really relax now. The heat that leads to a smile.

But that will lead to other things and a cracking sore head tomorrow. And that's not where he wanted to be tomorrow.

Slow Dancing In Hell

****

"Jesus Christ, look!" said Rob.

A young adult John Ford looked to Brian. He had taken the can from the table and ripped it open with his teeth.

"With his bare teeth!" he said. They laughed.

Then there was a drop of dark blood. *On the table.* On the table in front of them.

They were in a large group seated around some tables they had pulled together for the night out.

The drinking had started early, and everyone was in flying form.

Three of the lads were up dancing on the disco floor. Well it wasn't really what you could call dancing.

More a leaping about, flailing around with arms and legs in all sorts of uncoordinated actions. The more normal people backed away a little.

One guy had his two arms inside his jumper and was pumping it up and down, with the empty jumper arms flailing about the place like a cartoon from hell.

"Someone's put soap all over the disco floor…" whispered one of the lads to John. John looked and nodded. *Yep. Lot of slipping going on, on that dance floor.*

Pat was outside, thrown out by the door men. He was standing in the main street, surrounded by a group of passersby. They quickly stepped back when he vomited up his stomach onto the streets. Some mini dog cleaner robots were over to him, running around his feet and hoovering up the mess on the ground.

"The fuckin cheek of 'em." He said to the ground.

"Beer is like water in here…" he mumbled. The robot cleaner dog agreed with him heartily.

The music got much louder. Thumping bass beats. Getting faster and faster. A spiral of lights, and heat, dry mist and faster beats. The beer went down like water alright. The rain outside still fell. The neon lights outside grew bigger, larger, brighter. *The night charged on faster, faster.*

****

Otto's arm stretched out into the unknown. Into another set of worlds. His veins ran blood for a while, then it turned into something else.

"I'm not sure." Said Otto.

"Same here." Said Olivia. "At what exact point the blood begins to transform into whatever fluid it is that runs through the body of the other being. The being at the end of your arm."

"And how do I still stay alive?" he asked, on the table.

"Not sure. But I do think it is a crossover, a link that is more psychological, than physical. The subconscious is the reality here. Not us. So you are actually descending into your proper form. The real form you exist in within the subconscious. Not this human shell." Olivia was studying the hologram monitors on the screens around her. Her white lab coat was open slightly, the air in the room was warm. *Very warm.*

"I think you are becoming more real, than any of us ever have been." She said.

"Nice one Doc." He replied.

"No problem. Anytime." She replied.

"Will I be safe?" he asked.

"Does it rain in the desert every Tuesday?" she asked.

"Eh no." he furrowed his brow.

"Exactly." She nodded, continuing to examine the readouts.

The structure of the laboratory seemed to shift a little. *To twist a little in places. It was hard to see.* When she turned her head to it at any time, it seemed to revert back to its normal. *It was happening just out of sight.*

"What can you see now Otto?" she asked.

"Not much. It's quiet dark. I wonder if I am asleep ?"

"Nothing new there."

"Wait something is happening."

"What?"

"My eyes. I can see. Jesus."

"What?"

Otto stayed silent for a couple of minutes. Olivia watched the monitors closely. There were hints of pixelated images coming through. Shadows. It's a room of sorts. It's a dark, cold room. Perhaps a basement. Some green moss growing on the side walls. If they are walls. There is the sound of dripping liquid. Somewhere, echoing in the basement. The water dripped very slowly. One every twenty seconds or so. The building shape twisted a little. Olivia was starting to become accustomed to these reality shifts. *They don't seem to cause much of an issue. But they definitely occur. Not sure if it's the interface that is causing the issue, or if this is an actual regular occurrence in the subconscious. Or in the real. Or in someone's mind.*

"I have lots of eyes."

"What?"

"It's taking time to focus. Because I have lots of eyes. Thirty or so. Jesus I can see all around me. It feels so weird. I can't tell whats up , down , left or right."

"I'm getting some coordination on it now though."

Olivia waited, hands on hips, watching Otto on the table. He appeared asleep now. Not much movement.

"Can you see it on the screen…" He whispered.

"I am seeing one image. As usual. Nothing unusual. I can't tell from the image if there is one eye or a hundred eyes creating the image."

"Yes, well take it from me. That's my brain working overtime to figure it out and put it all into one image I think. But there's lots of them. All crystal clear."

"Go Otto!"

"It's like walking on the deck of a ship in very stormy weather."

"Very specific simile there Otto. Were you a sailor in a past life?"

"A sailor of broken hearts."

"Indeed."

"It's difficult to keep balance. So many images coming at me. I've started to learn how to see one or two or a few. To pick which is forward and go with that. Otherwise it is just too overwhelming."

"I seem to be reaching out for a door now."

"There's no stopping this man."

"Ugh."

"What?"

Another long silence.

"Sorry. It's tentacles. I'm all tentacles. It's… Jesus…."

She waits now. He's working on trying to process it all.

"I think I'm in a cell. A prison."

"What?"

"Yea. I think I'm a prisoner here. I can feel the unhappiness. The frustration. I can't get out of the door. The room. The one window is locked and barred. And it's a horrible place. And I, me, It knows this. It is not happy here."

Olivia tries to get more readings on the location, but it's impossible to pinpoint a place. "Our tech is based on our physical world. This is nothing it's seen before. It registers it like the insides of a dog. That is, it hasn't a fucking clue."

"It seems to call itself the dreamer."

"Nice."

"Its thoughts are very strange."

"Yet again, no surprises there."

"It says it has created all of this in a dream. In a nightmare. That it is not really a prisoner. But this dream had decided that he is a prisoner."

"More Otto more?"

"It says the dream had a mind. A consciousness of its own. And it is directing affairs. It is out of his control. And it does not like it."

"Can you ask it questions? Does it know you are there, is it aware of you."

"I don't think so. Not sure. It's thought processes are so different. It spins things around all the time. It is difficult to tell the end and the start. It's impossible to know really."

"Ask it."

"Ok I'll try."

Silence. Olivia checked the readings on the board this time. Nothing much. No real changes.

"It felt something alright. But seems to think I am an itch. A slight irritant. Like a low pain, a headache of sorts, that is growing. And not going away. I moved over to the window to see if it could focus on some activity to reduce the headache."

"Damn, it's bang on. It has you classified and diagnosed in seconds. These things must be intelligent so."

"There is no response to that."

"You are learning Otto."

4 DEEP DIVE

"God is Dead." - Friedrich Nietzsche

"When you stare into the abyss the abyss stares back at you."

- Friedrich Nietzsche

"So we have a thing, trapped in a prison. On the other end of your arm." Replayed Olivia. She pointed to the readout on the holographic screen in front of her. It hovered over Otto as well.

"Yes." He answered. "I think."

"And it's quite different than our candidate one creature. The previous predator in the forest." She nodded.

"Absolutely. Nothing like it at all."

"Could this be another location? Another segment of you, in another existence?" she asked.

"I suppose." Otto nodded. "It felt spider like. Lots of eyes. Lots of limbs. But with tentacles. Like some squid, spider crossover."

"Sounds like standard spider fear nightmare Otto. Could that be playing a part too?" she inquired.

"Not sure. I'm not particularly repulsed by spiders, or octopi. Not usually an issue. But then it is well known to be quite a regular phobia for people." He shrugged.

"But it said it was in a dream. And the dreamer, or the dream was in contact. That it too was alive?" she quizzed him.

"Yes. It said the dream though. Not the dreamer. At least I think that was it." He nodded.

"It was in a dream. So if we follow that line of thinking, it was not real. The dream was real. You were actually connected to the entity that called itself the dream. Not the spider thing." She suggested.

"Nah. Don't know about that. I was looking through a lot of eyes, and moving with tentacles. I felt like I was inside the creature. The prisoner." He explained.

"Hmmm." Said Olivia, stirring the coffee again.

"So we could be two layers deep in this one." She said.

"Possible." He grimaced.

"Or not." She added.

"Very possible." He shook his head.

"That's possible."

"That's possible too, that it's possible."

"It's all possible."

"That's very possible too."

Olivia nodded, finished the coffee and headed back to the lab. "Let's go see what's impossible so…" she said as she turned.

"Jesus…give me a minute…" he moved from his seat.

"Time is our enemy Otto." She snapped back.

"You are my enemy." He replied.

"I heard that…"

"Good…"

****

The Bathysphere descended deeper and deeper into the darkness. Down into the Plasma Pool. It was the darkest they had experienced yet. There was virtually no light outside. It didn't help that the external light system was also switched off to avoid attracting any of the locals down here.

"How deep are we now John?"

"Too fucking deep." He responded. "Way too deep."

"Very scientific John. What's the depth?"

"Around two million, fifty six Ks and increasing by 10ks every 2 seconds."

"Thanks."

"Do you think Otto will be ok?" Shauna asked Olivia, who was standing beside her as she watched the holographic readouts.

Olivia had her arms crossed. She reached out and lifted a cup of coffee. She sipped from the hot coffee. The steam rose up into the air. She paused.

"Hard to tell." She replied.

"He's talking again." She said.

"I'll do some more tests on him when he wakes up later on."

"Perhaps we are going too far, too quickly?" she asked Olivia.

"Isn't that the concept behind exploration?" asked Olivia.

"Maybe a more tactical approach, so that we still have our minds by the end of the journey, might be called for." Shauna looked to Olivia.

"We can slow it down alright. We are getting excellent data from Otto. And the cataloguing of creatures and structural mapping is moving at a fast rate." She answered quickly. The hologram colours reflecting off her eyes.

"The original estimate was to complete a small portion of a galaxy sized equivalent of data gathering within one year. That would allow us to analyse, and produce some further targets for deeper dives in year two." Continued Olivia, and paused to raise the coffee mug up.

"We have not yet gone down to our target depth yet for month 1. We are on target if we keep this pace and rate of dive, though. Including initial experiments with reach, psychology and senses." She added, sipping more coffee.

"True. On target. Going according to plan." Shauna looked to Olivia again. "But is it?" She asked.

"We have seen some strange things granted. We have experienced some stranger things. Granted. Nothing to concern though yet. Nothing unexpected." She replied.

Shauna looked into Olivia's eyes. For a second she thought she seen a coldness there. A rigidness not seen before. A steel shutter coming down.

"Really?" She tilted her head. *Maybe looking at me at a different angle might help*, thought Olivia.

"To be honest Shauna. I had expected a lot worse. Even after all the models were done, simulations and theories drafted. I expected us to be in deep trouble, mentally at least before the end of month one. I have never seen simulations and models stack up to reality. Particularly when it comes to the mind."

John turned around from his station to look at her.

"I expected John over here to be a gibbering baboon, Otto to burst into flames, and the rest of the crew to grow into plants…" she smiled, and sipped again.

"I see." Said John.

"But do you John? Do you?" she asked, smiling and staring back at him.

He laughed and turned back again to his station.

Shauna watched Olivia put the coffee cup down and walk away.

****

The videos and footage played on the screens step out from the holographic world and into the real world, while the craft was on low power running. Two soliders in uniform marched down the deck and then disappeared again. A snake slithered along the sink in the quarters of one of the crew.

Clouds and rain appeared within the medical lab.

****

"The liquid plasma is made up primarily from emotions." The computer explained.

Olivia and John stopped talking and listened.

The computer continued.

"The emotions are from all across the universe. Drifting around, randomly triggering events across the entire soup of life."

"Dream Eaters prowl the seas. Emotions are drawn from the pool. Emotions are eaten or drank with dreams."

"Here are some visuals of the human circulatory and nervous systems and how they interlink into a much larger network of neural networks across the universe."

"Pain triggering emotion is highly regarded in this universe."

"There are vast , unfathomable games of strategy and tactics played across these layered networks by immense beings. Too vast for us to understand on our tiny scale in comparison."

"These monstrous beasts that lumber through space and time are mindless, stupid and always destroying worlds, and populations of billions, in their search for more emotions and dreams."

"Akin to whales on earth, eating up plankton in the oceans, they open up and swallow huge sections of reality, swathes of dreams and emotions in one go."

****

"The clocks across the ship have been running backwards now for a day or so. It's very unnerving."

"Water tends to drip up towards the ceiling, even though there is no change in gravity across the craft."

"Maybe this is going too far."

"Maybe we are just only starting…"

Olivia and John held onto each other tightly as they made their way down through the deck of the craft. Sometimes the walls disappeared, sometimes the floor. Nothing was real. Everything was real too. The only thing that was real anymore was the both of them. Together. They held each other tight.

****

5 SINKING

'Who looks outside, dreams; who looks inside, awakes.'

– Carl Jung

"It's huge." Joan said. "The readings are suggesting it's at least a one hundred mile radius from the centre. And there appears to be some huge cathedral like building in the centre." She added.

"Can we get a better visual on it?" asked Shauna, stepping forward to the screen.

"Trying now." She repeated.

"Any lifeforms?" asked Shauna.

"Just the usual. Nothing new. Nothing appearing as intelligent." Joan replied.

"Ok. Not sure if that's good or bad. Big city, with no inhabitants." Added Joan.

"Good that we don't have to fight them. Bad that it is deserted." Said John.

"Why? How long? Any dating on the buildings?" asked Olivia.

"Appears to be built from plasma stone over hundreds of thousands of years ago. Readings suggesting at least, no wait…" Joan stopped. "Wow." She explained. She stared at the numbers on the screen in front of her.

"What?" Asked Olivia.

"Three billion years old and counting…" she explained, pointing at the readouts.

"What? No way!"

"Yes. That's it. Three billion."

"That's old." Said Shauna

"That's old." Said John.

"That's old." Said Otto.

"Is it old then?" asked Olivia.

They suited up and went out through the airlock. Swam down through the pool fluid and into the city.

It felt a bit like parachuting down into the city, thought Olivia.

They descended into a large open street. Down through the valley of giant, stone, skyscrapers. And past dead, old, burnt out, neon signs. On the streets below, vehicles were covered in moss and plant life which crept in and over the city walls. The vehicles were car like, but alien at the same time.

There were rows and rows of small apartments. "Possibly the inhabitants were more around the four foot tall mark or so." said John.

"Hobbit land." Said Olivia.

"The place is empty. No signals. No readings. It's been dead for a long time." Said Joan.

"Let's get inside that building over there. The big one. Looks like a business centre or such."

They drifted over the street. The jets in their suit packs guided them. And then touched down onto the streets. There was a green moss and plant growth everywhere.

It seemed like a combined business centre and a cathedral. It loomed over the street. The centre of the city perhaps. The epicentre.

The giant doors were slightly ajar. Enough to allow them to enter. They stepped inside. This was definitely not a four foot tall person building. The doors were at least fifteen metres tall. Like the entrance to an old castle on a mountainside in darkest Romania.

John pushed them open some more, just slightly, just enough so they could step through one by one easily. And to let some more light in.

Inside was a series of switches on the wall. Along the wall a series of light indicators circled the first chamber. The lights flickered on when they entered. A neon green colour lit up the walls.

"It's an airlock." Said John.

"Hit that one there, by you Olivia." He said.

Olivia clicked on one of the dots nearest to her. The doors closed behind them. The plasma fluid drained out of the airlock. When it was gone, the secondary doors opened towards them. They stepped inside. The airlock also removed all the plasma residue from their suits.

They were inside a huge chamber. Like a nave, the central area of a magnificent old cathedral. It was lit in green. It was a neon glowing green from some reflecting light sources. It rippled slightly, like the reflected surface of a pool.

Their helmets told them pressure was normal, oxygen was breathable. No dangerous viruses or bacteria in the area.

Olivia was the first to remove her helmet.

Then the others.

Any sound at all, the unbuckling of the helmets, a shift in feet, echoed deeply through the chamber. It was vast. And the ceiling was maybe a hundred metres above them.

"Is this materialisation from anyone here?" said Olivia, as she looked across the team.

"Nope."

"Don't recognise it." They all confirmed no.

"So it's not us."

"That's a 10 4." Said John.

She walked over to the nearest green neon glowing wall and touched it. "Feels real enough. But we all know that's not enough."

"There are libraries it appears." Said Joan, studying the readouts on her hand computer.

"And this is one of them." She continued.

Olivia raised her eyebrows. She walked on up through the centre of the chamber. There were control panels built into the walls on each side. She moved to the left, and she tried one green button. A huge hologram shot up beside her. She jumped quickly back.

It showed a plant. A large plant. And some writing or images underneath that she couldn't translate.

"Known language?" she asked.

"Not known." Said the computer in Joan's unit. The computers voice carried through their suit helmets.

****

"Can I control the dreamer?" she asked. Joan was lying on the medical lab table now. Her arms were connected into her cylinder.

Olivia was sitting on a stool at the main control desk over to her side. She explained.

"We don't know. That's one of the things we need to find out. How these links work. They can control you, we think. But only when they sleep, and you are active in their dream. But then, when you are active, or even not, can you use the link to control them? Or perhaps even communicate with them? Let's try shall we?"

"Let's do it" smiled Joan.

****

Joan sat in her bedroom, in her quarters, on the Bathysphere. She stared at the monitor in front of her. There were scenes from the street riots in the city on a large hologram.

"Zoom here." She ordered the computer. The screen responded by zooming into more detail.

"Here."

"Again here."

"Stop."

She looked on. She had a glass of wine in her hand. The screen showed Joan, in the middle of a group of friends. Charging at the riot police. They all wore school uniforms. She smiled.

She remembered they had taken the day off. They told their different school teachers they had to go to the dentist that day. Then travelled into the centre and joined up with the riot. There were thousands on the streets. Tens of thousands.

"They have finally done it." Said one of her friends.

"Yea." Said another.

"This time it is too much. How dare they ration the food! It's not like we are in a war or something." Joan added.

"Let's show them what we think!" said Gillie, the leader. She was tall and wore her hair in a long ponytail. The ponytail swung wildly from side to side when she spoke and when she walked.

She remembered that small town called Bellview on the borders of the city state, where she grew up. As soon as the local kids reached the ages of twelve and onwards, they would head into the city. The city was the place for work and for fun. For life. So gradually, the little town of Bellview grew old and the population declined. There were fewer travellers to the town.

The streets were empty. Old cars, and hover ships lined the main street. An empty hover port sat at the end of the main street. Two quiet bars kept their doors open, one on each side of the street. Some of the remaining men, fathers and grandfathers would drink there. Drink was the only entertainment in town. Her own father was fond of the 'A Sock For Every Shoe' bar.

Joan was known as a quiet kid around the town. She kept to herself, did her schoolwork and stayed in her bedroom a lot. Sometimes, she went out with the other kids. But would stay at the back. Always quiet, unobtrusive. She became known as the mouse within the school kids. *The mouse. I hated that name.*

When she got home from school she would lose herself in her books. Alice in wonderland. The Phantom Tollbooth, Harry Potter and the Earthsea trilogy. To name a few.

Joan was not as tall as the others, around five foot three when she was about eighteen.

Joan lived with her father and mother. Until her father left. *Which was no bad thing* she thought, sipping from the wine glass.

Men, She thought. *Do we really need them? Nowadays.* She shook her head. *It didn't seem that way.*

On the way to the riots. They walked quickly, skipped here and there. Sang one of the latest pop songs. At one stage, the five of them linked arms as they walked, skipped their way along the main road. They kicked out their legs like show girls. *Marching forward.*

Joan dreamt of a big house. *With lots of cars. And a swimming pool. And some nice boys around. But nothing permanent.* She didn't like permanent. *It was too much obligation.*

Joan thought of how they would survive without their father. This was long before he ever left. She had begun thinking that way from quite a young age. He was drunk most days. And he just didn't really exist in her world. *He was just there.* She had long given up trying to connect with him. *It was a bit like trying to connect with a brick. Occasionally, when you touch it you might get a different reaction, if it was a hot day, it would be warmer. Or if someone had moved it, it might look different. But mostly it responded like a brick. With no response at all.*

She wondered *if it was her*. And she kind of knew *it was her. An unexpected child. Landed straight in the middle of a promising young career of a young manager.* And then bang. She came along. *And blew everything up. Well probably not everything. A seven pound baby rarely does that itself.* The world was blowing up around him anyway. *But he just couldn't distinguish one thing from another. Cause or effect was out of his reach. Only the bottle.*

But she knew it was her. She knew the bitterness stemmed from her. From her arrival on the scene. *Never spoken. Never said out loud. Never referred to. Like a feeling in the back of your head. You know it is true. It is true. But you never talk about it. Like you know a person in school just doesn't like you. Or you know that you will not be that person you want to be. It's there. All the time.*

Joan knew she would never have the house, the cars or the pool. For some reason. This was just a known fact to her. And so, her father sat and watched holograms all day when he was in the house. And she would wander in and out. *Try, and give up. And often try. And give up again.* Until she stopped trying. *It was easier that way. Stop trying.*

She remembered the march that day. The riot police. All in black. Armed with holo-shields. And guns. She remembered staring at the guns. At the men in armour. There were very few women in armour. *Probably had more sense.*

Her father had left. *Well, to be more correct, hadn't been seen in the house for about two years at this stage now.* She was sixteen staring at the riot police. She thought of the empty chair by the hologram player in the sitting room. *Fuck him*, she thought then. And stared at the police.

The riot police charged at them. They drew their weapons and fired. People dropped like flies around her. One of her friends dropped first. *Then another. Fell, hit the ground.* The crowd were screaming and shouting. *The crowd were running now backwards. In all directions.* She turned and ran back. She thought of her friends on the ground. *Gillie. Dead. Michelle. Dead.*

She ran down the main street. With hundreds of others all around her too. *Running and shouting.* The banners dropped on the ground. *The fight gone.*

On the side of the dusty road she sat. Her head was in her hands. Her clothes marked with blood. Her uniform. There were bodies on the ground up ahead of her. Nearer the city gates.

The gates were closed now.

She looked at those gates. The closed gates of the city. *The huge metropolis. Of wealth. Of the streets paved with gold. Of the swimming pools inside. And the cars. And the money. The clothes. The labels. The boys. The men. The dreams.*

She shook her hair out. The dust was everywhere. And stared at those city gates.

A single tear ran down her face. Down her cheek, and slowly, through the dust covered face, and down around under her jaw. Gone. She waited and waited.

She wiped the trail of the tear off her dusty face. Stood up. And began the long walk home.

Slowly.

****

"I can see something." Said Joan. Eyes closed. Arm wired into her cylinder.

"What?" said Olivia.

"It's…. It's…."

"Take your time, let the signals come. It will eventually get clearer. Your brain will sort it all out."

"It's a tank. Like a cylinder but much bigger. I am… It is inside the tank."

"Ok. Good. Can you describe it? Let's see if we can get visuals going on screen…"

"It's a big tank. But I'm inside. Looking out. There are bubbles of gas, oxygen maybe in the tank running up the fluid around me."

"I'm attached to things. Inside the tank."

"It's hard to breathe. It's hard to think."

"Take your time. It will take time to connect. It will take time for reality there to become real to your brain."

"I can feel the straps. I am strapped onto a cross or something in this tank."

"I am hot. Very hot."

"I can taste salt in my mouth. I think."

"I think it's my mouth."

On the hologram screen in front of Olivia, the bubbles drifting up in the tank begin to appear. The glass of the tank appears. The outside room that the tank is positioned in starts to become clear. It's empty. It's clear.

"It is dreaming about me." She said.

"OK… ok. It's just a dream…let it roll."

On the screen, the riot police appear clearly. The gates of the city open. The people on the streets.

"It's me, when I was young. With my friends…"

"Is it dreaming this? Is it dreaming this into reality?"

"Not sure Joan. Let's keep going…"

On the screen, the crowd are warming up. Chanting and waving placards. The view is slightly behind Joan's head in the scene.

"I hate this…"

"It's just an image now Joan. It's not real. Not that we understand it to be."

"They will die…"

"Who?"

"Gillie, Michelle. My friends. They will die…"

Olivia stopped reviewing the hand held computer and looks up at the hologram screen in front of her.

"I don't want them to die…" Joan pleaded from the table. Eyes still closed.

"This is the dreamer Joan." Said Olivia.

"This is the dreamer that dreams you. That makes your reality." Olivia said it slowly. Carefully.

"No!" shouted Joan.
"Yes. This is your demented guardian angel. Your God. Here in this tank in a laboratory somewhere."

"No. Olivia No."

"This creature is another nerve ending from something else. It probably doesn't even know it is dreaming. It is just generating a reality. It's a dream for him, for it. But it's our reality."

"My head hurts." Said Joan.

"Same here." Said Olivia, looking around for a pen to use on her computer display.

"I will try to talk to it, to communicate with it." Said Joan.

"Ok. Ok. Good." Said Olivia staring at the screen.

"Thing." Joan says quietly.

"Thing in a bottle. Listen to me. Listen. You do not want this. This is not good…"

Something happened on the screen. The image began to twist and turn a little just a little. Olivia frowned.

"Make it stop." Joan whispered, as if talking to a little baby.

The image crackled a little. The figures around Joan on screen began to fade away. The city faded away into the dust. The riot police faded away.

After several minutes. Joan was left standing alone in the middle of the dusty street. She just stood there. Staring ahead. She looked at the very spot where the riot police stood. But there was nothing but dust now. Nothing.

Beside her, on the ground a particularly hairy big spider walked slowly along just by her foot. She moved her foot, stepped then to the side a little, to let him go by.

"He heard me." Said Joan.

"Yes. Yes it did." Replied Olivia, as she watched the screen.

"I feel different." Said Joan.

"In what way?"

She thought for a moment. Then replied.

"I feel lighter. I feel that Gillie and Michelle are ok now. I feel I am ok now. I don't feel sad. Somewhere. Somewhere I used to feel sad. But it's not there anymore."

"Good."

"What is this? Is this real."

"Truly. I haven't the faintest idea."

"We are cut off from the main universe now. There is no communications back and forth. There is no way to tell if we effected any changes back in our reality." Said Olivia, as she helped Joan stand up from the table.

They both unhooked the various cables and connectors to the cylinders and Olivia handed Joan a cup of coffee.

"Thanks." She said, and sipped.

"That's good. That's so good." She smiled.

"It felt like it was real. If you know what I mean. Like it happened that way."

"Very likely. That creature dreams you. It dreams your past, present and future. So if it undreamed a section of your past. It is likely that section is now gone. Removed from our reality."

"That Gillie and Michelle are not dead?"

"Possible. Difficult to confirm but possible."

"That's just pure magic."

"I know, isn't it?" Smiled Olivia.

"It's just the tip of the iceberg Joan. Just the start."

"It sounds creepy though. What else could you do with this? This could change people forever."

"Well, we have to wait and see. Not sure. Nothing is sure here. That thing, could just re-dream the original again in the next ten minutes, or tomorrow, and it's back to where it was. It's in the tank creatures hands, or tentacles. Not a good feeling to be in the control of someone else huh?"

"Yea exactly." Joan sipped again from the hot coffee. "Or sometimes we allow ourselves to be controlled by those around us. And we could actually stop it at any time, but we are choosing not to. To avoid the scene. The confrontation. The fallout."

"Yes. For various reasons, real and imagined, people often stop themselves from tackling the real trouble in life. The real blockers."

****

 "One theory has it that there is a theatre. A huge theatre. Where the dreams of the dream demons are played out. In our case, it was our universe. Our world. But occasionally the dreams occur in other realms or universes. Hence, people can be transferred from one realm to another. From one dream reality to another." Olivia poked at the fried egg on her plate in front of her. John, Joan, Shauna and Otto sat around the table as well, eating their lunch.

"This giant theatre is like a shared, online, open world, adventure game.

The beasts that dream, wired up to it…their dreams of us running constantly." She continued, moving the egg into the centre of her plate and pointing at it.

"We play out various stories and themes to their will. To the will of their subconscious. Which as we can see with ourselves, are often not in line with the actual wants and will of the conscious creature." She moved her beans to various positions around the egg.

"These creatures are not gods. They are dumb. Some insane. Some housed in experimental tanks. Some living ordinary lives like our own. Some are aware and behave like Gods over realms. Some drift into and out of the dreams of others." She positioned the salt and pepper container outside on the rim of her plate. One on each side of the plate.

"Nasty."

"Yes. It is. Or at least it's some kind of model that our minds can understand in some way. It's more than likely wrong. And riddled with holes. But it's a hell of a lot more than we knew say five years ago."

"We are starting to peel away the layers of the onion. We are only at the top, the surface. But we are starting to see below the waterline."

"To see the rest of the iceberg underneath."

****

Joan entered the medical lab. She was on her own. She prepared the desk holograms. And settings. The central examination table slowly turned around into position. The tentacles in the cylinders at the back of the room moved when she entered. They touched at the glass. They wanted out. They wanted to be free. Joan climbed onto the table and attached herself up to the tentacles in her cylinder.

She lay back.

"Computer Begin." She said.

She had pre-loaded the scenario she wanted into the computer in the privacy of her own room earlier.

On the hologram screen hovering above her an image began to appear.

Her eyes closed and she turned her head to the side on the table.

A small house appeared on the screen. On a dusty road. In a town far outside the main gates of the city gates. The sitting room was buzzing with the loud noise of a hologram show in the centre of the room.

The house was empty. There was one person sitting in the armchair by the hologram. There were empty beer bottles and whiskey bottles by the chair. An open pizza box, and half a slice of pizza on the table. Flies buzzed around the pizza.

Her father was asleep in the chair. His head was turned to the side. His breath laboured. The hologram show boomed on regardless. Some mindless lottery show. Bet a thousand dollars and win a billion the attractive lady on the screen hollered out.

A twitch ran down the side of her father's face. Like a nerve spasm. His mouth opened a little…

Joan moved on the lab med table. She was in deep now. *Down deep. Living the dream.*

She ran towards him. Towards the back of his head in the armchair. She ran screaming. She pushed him. His head. And hit. And hit. And beat and beat. Over and over again.

She turned around the chair then and face on, pummelled his face. It began to run red. The eyes running down his face. Onto his chest. Into his lap. The head coming apart like an egg.

She smashed and smashed. Until there was nothing left. Just a pool, a mess of things on the floor. A goo.

She stopped. Breathless. And stepped back. "Fuck you." She said. Quietly.

She turned and walked back out to the kitchen. On her way, she called to the holo tv. "Switch off."

The screen faded into nothing.

Her body lay on the medical lab table. Her hand twitched. Her leg twitched. It was like she was having a bad dream. The floating hologram screen projected images of the blood red floor across the room.

6 DROWNING IN MAGIC

"Knowing your own darkness is the best method for dealing with the darknesses of other people."

– Carl Jung

It was the beginning of month four. Shauna looked across the table at Joan. The team were starting to look a bit rugged. Unkempt might be another word for it. But that's ok. We weren't here to be pretty. Yes but we need to be professional. On top of our game. Ready for anything. Fit. Alert. Motivated. Yes this is also true. So much is true. What is important? That's the question. Shauna crossed her arms and stared at Joan.

"It's wonderful." Said Joan.

"It's so liberating." She smiled and nodded. "I could just plug in. And see what he sees. And seen my past, and stuff. And I could just do what I wanted. I can change shit."

"It's like reliving a memory, but the way you want to relive it."

"That's it. Nothing else. I came out of it fine. I could disconnect and walk away. It just felt like I had the greatest sleep ever. Like my dreams had figured out shit and done it the way it should have been done. And that's it."

"Can you talk to it?"

"To?"

"The dreamer?"

"No. I haven't really tried yet. I think he or it knows I'm there though. How else could it let me know the things I want to do."

"Has he stopped anything you wanted to do?"

"No. Nothing. No interference at all. I don't think he cares really. He's probably busy building other worlds in another dream space or something."

"Or maybe he's in a coma."

"Or maybe dead."

"So, what we are saying here is that we can somehow connect with a dreamer. Who is dreaming us into reality, is that it? Then adjust the dream to our liking. We can do what we need to do. But does this change our reality?"

"It sure feels like it." Said Joan.

"Is your father dead now, in reality?" asked Otto.

"I think so."

"Wow."

"That's murder."

"Is it? If I am in charge of the dream. And this is only a dream. Then how is it murder? Murder is killing something real. Something with a physical presence."

"So we are not real now?"

"Pretty much not."

"That's a fairly substantial leap."

"Could I go into a dream state then, and kill you in the dream state? And when I awake, you are dead. And things just go on?" Shauna's mouth was open. Her eyes wide.

"When I seen him. It was as if I was five years old again. It was definitely in the past. He was at that stage. He was probably around thirty two or something. The house was exactly as it was, when I was that young. I was in the past."

"But it suggests you, or anyone could do it now."

"But you could do that now. You wouldn't need to go via the dream guy to kill me now. What would be the point of that? You could just lift that knife now and stab me here." Joan pointed to her heart.

"Might be a good idea." Said Otto.

"Just try it." She stared at him.

"I'm confused." Said George.

"Not the only one." Said Joan.

"Ok let's conduct an experiment." Said Olivia.

"Say we get a mouse from the lab. And we put him in a cage over there. Then we get Joan to hook into the cylinder. In her dream, she can pour some dye on the mouse. Then we go check the mouse and see what has happened."

"It can't happen."

"Why?"

"Because Joan is on the table. She will have to get up from the table and go to the mouse to do it. This will disconnect her from the dream."

"Oh yes."

"So we need Joan to get into the dream and manipulate someone else to pour dye on the poor mouse."

"Yes. That might work."

"So it worked with her father, because it was old her. Past her. Not present her. Somehow she could access the past her and do it. But doing anything to disconnect her from the dreamer would stop it of course. So present her could not do anything while connected."

"Is it possible to manipulate other people in this plane? Perhaps only herself."

"We will see."

"I would think only the dreamer can manipulate anyone else. Why would she have the ability to move me around on the chessboard here?"

"True."

"Can you influence the dreamer?" Otto asked.

"Good question. It doesn't seem to allow me to communicate with him. Although we have tried. It could be that it just doesn't respond. It may actually feel and understand us."

****

Joan's room was quiet. There wasn't a sound from outside or in. The holograms and systems were on sleep mode for the night. There was a green light flashing in the far corner, ready for input if needed. A single, solitary, token available for anyone to be sure the systems were still available, but asleep. A comfort light.

Each crew member had their own personal quarters on board the Bathysphere. The individual cabins contained a sitting room, a kitchen area, dining area, bathroom and bedroom. They were identical in shape, layout and furniture. The walls and flow were bathed in a neon glow, a navy blue. There were many ancient patterns, superstitions and symbols projected on the walls via holographic projectors built into the walls, floors and ceiling. The dimmed lights were relaxing. And the lighting and wall coverings were completely configurable by the crew on a whim. Their personal AI systems managed all room settings.

The kitchen provided a small unit for cooking, drinks, cupboards, a small table and a sink for any cutlery and dishes. Functional. Nothing more. It used the same lighting and decorating systems as the rest of the cabin.

The bathroom was well equipped and bathed in an aquamarine lighting.

The bedroom was large, dark and just a hint of neon blue glow. The bed was a large king size. Joan turned over in the silk cover. The cover was light, but the room was warm. The room systems maintained the right temperature and air conditioning settings based on Joan's body indicators.

Joan's thoughts were clearer now. She thought about undersea diving. She thought about how great it would be to swim in the seas of ancient Earth. *The training that was required. Swimming off the coast of some gorgeous island in the Mediterranean Sea, with a crystal blue water sea, and a golden beach.*

A huge spiked tentacle slithered slowly up the silk bedsheet. It reached up and slid around her neck. It wrapped gradually around her head and face. Until her neck and face were entirely covered. The skin was like a reptile. But wet too. There were smaller creatures, little, lice like creatures crawling around the surface skin of the tentacle. They hopped from the tentacle onto Joan's face and into her hair.

She made a slight muffled noise. But was still asleep.

The slimy tentacle continued to wrap itself around the entire bed. A second tentacle was sliding across the floor. Another one reached out across the wardrobe. It touched the wardrobe, and the door automatically opened. It slid inside, brushing off over her clothes.

The movement sensors kicked in and the internal computer flickered on. The green light stopped flashing and switched fully on. Two hovering drone cameras turned on.

Joan slept on.

The creature sounded like someone slurping with a straw from the bottom end of a soft drink cup in a cinema. It echoed around the room, slow and prolonged.

The tiny creatures that crawled on the tentacles ran across the bed covers and down onto the floor. They were in her drinking cup. They were in the bathroom. Inside the wardrobe. More and more poured out from the surface of the tentacles. Like an army of ants.

The drone cameras buzzed on, light indicators remained on green.

****

Joan was up early. She was in the shared workout area. She stretched out on a matt on the floor and stretched her legs. She was alone.

The drone cameras buzzed around her.

"Play some classical." She said to her own AI. Some soothing soft violins drifted around the room.
"Nice…." She smiled. She moved to doing some press ups.

"Any news?" she asked the air.

"Nothing much yet." The AI replied.

"Fair enough."

"Joan?" came Shauna's voice over the sound system.

"Yes?" she stopped after another press-up.

"Can you drop over to me? I've got something on footage to show you." Said Shauna.

"Sure – thirty minutes?"

"I think you might want to see this now…" she said.

"Oh ok. On my way."

Joan knocked on Shauna's door. Shauna called out to her."One Sec."

The door opened. In the living room area of Shauna's quarters, the hologram screen was frozen on a camera view of Joan's bedroom.

"What's up boss?" asked Joan, entering the room.

"Here, sit down." Shauna handed her a glass of water. "It's water. Don't worry." She said.

"This is going to be a shock, Joan. Prepare yourself please." Shauna placed her hand on Joan's shoulder. Joan stared at her. Shauna nodded and pointed to the chair.

Joan sat into the chair. It was metallic, a wireframe curved seat. It bent backwards to take her frame.

"Play." Shauna instructed the AI.

On the hologram screen, which grew larger for two to view now, the camera was focussed on a sleeping Joan.

"Ok …nice… maybe you could've asked me out for dinner first…" smiled Joan.

"Much easier this way. I can get to know you, before you get to know me…" said Shauna.

"Creepy."

"That's not the half of it…" Shauna replied.

The huge tentacle crept along from the floor and up onto the bed. It moved slowly across.

Joan sat and stared.

It slithered gradually up around her neck and her head. And wrapped itself around her head. She held her breath and froze in the chair.

She put the glass of water down on the nearby neon blue table.

"Freeze." Said Shauna.

Joan stood up, in Shauna's quarters and stared at the hologram.

"Is this real footage?" said Joan. She already knew the answer.

"Yes." Shauna looked at her. She put her hand on her arm. "It doesn't appear to have done any real physical damage to you at all. The physicals from your medical monitoring AI all come out fine."

"Christ." Whispered Joan.

"It appears to want to wrap around you. To be with you. To hug you. We think." Whispered Joan.

"Nice." Said Joan.

"Yea I know…consent…" said Shauna.

"What the fuck is it?" she asked both Shauna and the AI.

"Presence unknown." Said the AI.

"That." Said Shauna.

"Did you feel or notice anything?" said Shauna.

"Nothing. Absolutely nothing. I was asleep…" she replied, holding her hair back.

"I… I got up this morning as usual, went for a workout, as usual…nothing. I feel I had a great night's sleep alright. Well rested. Ready for action. Ready to do one hundred press ups to be honest. Like a bright spring morning and a day off all ahead of me."

Shauna looked at her. She moved in closer and looked at her neck. Nothing. Not a mark. Nothing.

"Play it back." Said Joan.

The hologram turned slightly so she could view it from the seat better. The tentacle crawled up the bed.

"Stop. Zoom in."

The scene exploded outwards on the screen. "Again in."

The surface of the skin of the creature was scaly, but hard, like a lizard. And wet. Slippery. There was a pool of fluid along the tentacle, like a trapped puddle in the branch of a tree. There were spikes around the pool. There were suckers, just like an octopus.

"Again."

"Jesus." Said Joan.

On the screen were some of the tiny lice like creatures moving up and down the tentacle.

"Continue." Said Joan.

It played on.

****

"There are constant tales of creatures, images, visitors in the night in psychological interviews. And in the literature." Olivia re-watched the footage on her screen.

"There are several possible theories. It's the dreamer. It's another Plasma Pool creature. It's a manifestation from your own subconscious. It's John dressed up in a Halloween outfit…" She tapped the desk in front of her.

"Any of these are likely…" and looked at Joan directly.

"Thanks Olivia." Joan smiled.

"You're welcome." Olivia continued…

"But more importantly, what the fuck are those little creatures that ran all over the room…" said Olivia.

"What the hell were you drinking last night? And were you near the tank and cylinder at all?"

"Nothing, no and no" said Joan.

"It might be aware of you now. Now that you travelled and connected with it. It wasn't too happy where it was. It might see you as a way out. Or it might just want to talk to you. It also suggests it may have formed some sort of connection with you."

"Great." Said Joan.

"Or it may want to use you, or eat you. There are so many options really. We really don't know enough to start to eliminate the options and get to the heart of this."

"So monitoring tonight?"

"Yes. Or we can induce sleep now and see if something happens?" said Olivia.

"Let's do it now. I don't want this thing on me again." Said Joan.

"Ok. Meet in the lab in ten minutes. Let me get dressed here and sorted. Actually make it twenty." Olivia replied, picking up the cups and moving to the kitchen.

"Ok."

****

"Ready?" said Olivia.

They were in the Med-lab. Joan was on the medical table. The holograms all showed normal body readings and life signs.

"Sure." Said Joan, sighing.

"In ten…" said Olivia. "AI, run this through and make sure we have full monitoring on the brain and nervous system please."

"Yes." Said the AI.

****

Olivia watched the monitor as the psych readings showed Joan had entered a sleep.

Within seconds, giant tentacles materialised all over the Med-lab.

One grabbed Olivia before she could say or do anything.

The tentacle lifted her up, shook her around like a twig and let her go. She hit the ground hard.

The tentacles reached out, slithered across the floor and over to Joan on the medical table. They climbed up the sides of the table. They slid over Joan and wrapped around her tightly. She was breathing. But only just.

Some of them wrapped around Olivia, lying on the ground. She struggled to shake them off but they were too strong. Like giant python snakes. They held her tight.

Joan whispered in her sleep. "Open Doors." And the Med-lab doors slid open. The cameras are still recording all of this.

The tentacles begin to grow out into the corridor, through the doorway. Out into the surgically clean neon blue corridor.

Shauna was walking down the corridor towards the medlab. She turned the corner and a huge tentacle was crawling towards her on the floor. She turned and ran back towards the bridge. "What the fuck!" Shauna shouted.

She slammed the door behind her.

"There's a fucking alien crawling down the corridor outside. Are none of the sensors picking this up?" she shouted.

"Nothing on the sensors." Said the computer. John and Otto looked over at her, standing at the door, in surprise.

"Get some guns. Flamethrowers. Do we have any acid? Any poison?" she said, heading for the armoury.

John and Otto followed. "Otto stay here at the bridge. We will need some comms. Keep the fuckers out of here at all costs."

"Sure." Replied Otto.

"John follow me."

"Roger."

"And don't call me Roger."

"Roger."

She smiled as she ran to the armoury. "What is it?" he asked behind her. "Fucked if I know. Looks like one of those things from Joan's dreams. And it doesn't look friendly."

They pulled down a rifle each.

The bridge door slid open and Shauna and John stepped out.

The entire corridor was full of tentacles. They grew from the floor, from the walls and ceiling. They lashed about, wildly. The tentacles dripped fluids everywhere.

"Plasma?" said John.

"Probably… I hope" she replied.

The tentacles immediately reacted to their presence. The creatures began to detach from the walls and ceiling and move toward Shauna and John.

"Jesus." Said Shauna. John raised his gun.

"Wait. Don't hit the hull. A rupture could kill us all." Said Shauna.

"Then what the fuck good are these things?" said John.

"There's a flame thrower on it. Choose option 2." Said Shauna.

One of the tentacles grabbed Shauna and slammed her down onto the floor. She dropped her rifle.

John reached to help her. Another one grabbed him. Then another one. They wrapped around him and squeezed him hard.

Two more tentacles now grabbed onto him. He could feel his arms getting pulled out to their lengths.

"Option 2." Said John.

The gun settings clicked. He turned it and pulled the trigger.

The flames engulfed the bottom half of the tentacle. The tentacle retracted from him and let him go.

He moved the flames towards the base of the other tentacle. It burned quickly and fell away.

More tentacles moved in on him now.

The burned one split into other smaller tentacles and crawled back towards him.

"Holy shit!" he pointed the rifle at them and burned. The flames ripped through the corridor. Some of them hitting the bottom of Shauna's foot. She was entirely covered in tentacles.

He burned the remaining ones off himself. At this stage, Shauna had freed the rifle and pulled the trigger. Two bullets ripped into a tentacle around her leg. The tentacle let go, and began splitting into smaller tentacles.

"Option 2!" she called out. Her rifle reset.

She sat up. Two of the tentacles were still spiralling around her body and up to her neck. She pointed the gun at the base of the tentacles, near the walls and floor. Shauna pulled the trigger. The flames shot out of the rifle and the tentacles lit up in fire. The flames danced around the corridor. She pulled herself along the floor, over to John, back towards the bridge door.

"Come on! Come on John!" she said, reaching out for him. He was covered in little tentacles now. Too small to use the flamethrower on without doing himself some serious damage. Blood was oozing out from his legs. He crawled in behind her.

"They're eating me!" he screamed."Jesus, get them off!" He frantically ripped at the smaller creatures now crawling all over his legs.

"Open Door!" she screamed. "Open now! Fucks sake!"

The door slid open.

"Close!" the bridge door slammed shut behind them. Otto stared at them, both on their knees.

"Do we have anything we can fire at these things that won't breach the hull?" She said, as she lay on the floor with John. Otto reached down to help them. He stopped when he seen the smaller tentacles all over John's legs.

Otto pulled the creatures from John. One by one. They were attached, like leeches, to John's legs. John grabbed at them too. Shauna managed to stand up again, and checked her burnt foot. Not too bad. Shoe was burnt. Nothing else.

They stomped on the smaller tentacles, squashing them into the floor. Tiny bits of plasma shot out everywhere.

Otto looked up at the holographic screens around the bridge. The cameras were showing the tentacle creatures now. But the sensor equipment was not picking up any signs of them. The tentacles were all over the corridor now outside the bridge. It was a nest of them. Like a jungle of living squirming tentacles.

"They are replicating! Fuck, it looks exponential…" He stared at the expanding data on the line curve in front of him.

"Get some medical supplies – some bandages. We have to stop the bleeding." Demanded Shauna.

Otto ran to the emergency supplies unit at the back of the bridge.

"What the fuck was all that about?" said John.

"We have to wake Joan up…I think it's from her. From her mind, her dreams or something!" said Shauna.

"Olivia?!" she shouted into space.

"Yes – Shauna. I'm on my way."

"Don't come near the bridge. The corridor is infested with creatures. I want you to see what you can do with Joan. I think these things are coming from Joan's head. Or something fucking weird like that."

"Sure, I'm on it."

"Don't go to the Med-lab. It's covered with them too."

The hull of the Bathysphere made a loud noise. Like something really big and nasty was squeezing it tightly.

"Shit, what's that?" said John. "Let me check." He climbed up to a nearby desk station to see the external monitors.

Otto returned with a small red box with supplies. "John, put these on. Come here." He said. John slid back down onto the floor. There was blood all over the floor, walls and door. He didn't feel much pain from it.

"Why am I not feeling any pain… What's happening?"

"God fucking knows." Said Shauna.

Otto went to wrap a white strip of bandage around John's leg wound, near the calf. Just as he moved the bandage over him, a tentacle reached out from inside John's leg. It reached for Otto and grabbed his hand. The bandage fell to the floor. Otto grabbed it with his other hand and pulled it free. He pulled and pulled, and it finally detached from John's leg and he fell back. He dropped it on the ground and stood on it. There was nothing left but small bits of flesh, and a pool of liquid on the floor.

Otto went back to applying the bandage.

"Wait!" said John. "Maybe there's more inside me?" Otto stopped. He reached back into the kit and took out a small scanner device.

"Computer" Otto said. "Can you see these things inside John, can you display on the main screen please."

A detailed chart of John's body appeared on the screen. Another tentacle appeared to grow out of the wound on the calf. More blood seeped out.

There was nothing showing on the scan. "Computer you are not registering that creature. That fucking thing crawling out of his leg right now!"

"What thing?" said the computer.

Otto stared at Shauna.

She shook her shoulders and retuned to scanning the images of the corridor.

"The cameras were showing the tentacles, so they are physical entities.

Reality. They are actually there." She said out loud.

"But the AI systems aren't registering the creatures at all. They don't sense them. Or feel them… I don't know."

"Otto?" said Olivia, from her quarters.

"Yes. I hear you."

"Adjust the tuning on the AI scanning equipment to monitor the Plasma Pool frequencies dimension please."

"But it will not see any of us, or anything in the real world."

"Fuck the real world, we are well beyond that now. Do it!" shouted Olivia.

Otto climbed back over to the main console before the screen at the centre of the bridge.

He moved some levers, and hit some nice colourful readouts on the holo-panel in front of him.

"Display view of John now, with Plasma Pool parameters."… The screen changed.

"Holy Shit!" Otto stepped back from the screen.

"What the fuck!" said Shauna.

"Computer, relay charts to the medlab and my quarters too please." Demanded Olivia.

"Lord god…" was the only whispered sound that came from Olivia's channel.

■■■

On screen was a visual graphical representation of John's body. In a rough outline that was close to a human body, thousands of squirming, grabbing, snatching tentacles were crawling around.

The scene was a nightmare.

The entire crew looked at the scene on the screen in front of them.

John looked up at the monitor. Blood still seeping from his leg onto the floor.

"John!" came the shout from Olivia's monitor. "I'm going down there now! John! Jesus!"

"Don't!" shouted Shauna. "Olivia! Don't. The corridor is full of them. Otto relay it. There is no way into here!"

Images of the corridor appeared on the the screens in the bridge, in the medlab. The screens were filled with these tentacle creatures crawling and twisting all over one another.

"Jesus! John!" She shouted.

Otto turned to look down on John. A tentacle creature crawled out of his left eye. Its swirling, reaching tentacle twisted around and about. And then another one.

His skin began to burst. The creatures were bursting out of his arms now. Out of his legs…

His mouth opened…. "Oliv…." Was all he could get out. They crawled out of his mouth now. Out of his ears. Out of his pores.

They were spreading now on the deck of the bridge. Crawling around. *Looking for more hosts.*

"Joan! Wake up for fucks sake!" screamed Olivia on the speaker.

"Computer, wake Joan Lee in the Med-lab immediately!" shouted Olivia. Olivia was inside the protected room in the medlab. Behind the main screen.

"There is a risk that it can cause damage to the nervous system, if a subject is…"

"Wake her the fuck up now!" shouted Olivia.

One of the holo panels showed a view of the Med-lab. It was crawling with these tentacles. They were much larger now. Knocking cases and glasses over in the lab.

On a circuit board, it showed a charge of blue lightning running down through the circuits and hitting Joan's connectors.

She turned on the medical table. She swung her head back and forth.

On another holo-screen, John's body was decaying as the creatures spread out from his centre. It was no longer holding the shape of a human body.

Shauna looked down at him, they were falling off him like sores from a leper. John couldn't focus his thoughts. His mind wandered. *The tentacles were like a castle made of ants, but the ants were leaving now, and the walls were decaying. Everything was decaying. Very slowly. Like a stop motion video of a decaying plant.*

"Joan!! Joan!!! WAKE UP!!!" screamed Olivia.

"Again computer! Hit her again. Hit her with an electric shock. Get her awake now!" she shouted.

"She's not responding." Answered the computer.

"Fuck this!" Olivia slammed the desk against the wall, turned to the kitchen area, grabbed a chopping knife from the counter and stormed into the main medlab area.

"Olivia no!" shouted Shauna.

On the holo-panels above. They could see the tentacles and beasts crawling around the insides of the Bathysphere.

On other panels, which remained tuned to reality, they could see Olivia as she made her way down the corridor from medlab monitoring room to the main Med-lab. On the sensor panels, it looked like she was fighting and cutting her way through nothing but air.

On the screens attuned to the creatures, the invaders were sliced and cut apart. Bits of their internals, and their fluid was flying everywhere. An invisible enemy was slicing them to ribbons.

They grabbed at her, at the knife, but she pushed through.

One grabbed her by the leg. A huge one. She reached down with the knife and sliced at it. She sliced off pieces of it until it began to loosen grip. At the same time another one winded down from the ceiling and had wrapped itself around her neck.

She reached up with the knife. She paused quickly and prepared. And sliced. She cut through and it too fell off. Carefully, without getting her neck.

The lab door shot open. Inside was a jungle of these creatures. Crawling out of the walls. Crawling along the ceiling. Dropping down into her hair. Onto her clothes and around her feet. She charged towards Joan, who was asleep on the main table.

One grabbed her around the leg. Then another. Then another. They pulled her down. She hit the ground with a slap. Hard. Her head against the side of the table. Olivia pulled herself up slowly, all the while more of them crawled all over her. She pulled herself up to the level and shook Joan. Shook her hard. "Joan!" she called out. "Joan!" She shook and shook.

Joan turned. She made a moaning noise. Olivia reached over and pulled the connectors off Joan's arm. "Joan!" she screamed. She shook her hard. She slapped her hard. Joan moaned loudly. She punched her in the face. One of Joan's eyes opened. Then another.

"Joan come on!!!!!Fuck it!!!"

Joan sleepily came around. She pushed herself up on the table, and looked around. Olivia grabbed a container of water on a nearby table, out from the clutches of the tentacles, who appeared to be slowing a little now. They were fading a little. She threw the water over Joan's face. Her eyes were wide open now. The sting of the cold water. She was awake. Alert.

"Joan!!!" called out Olivia. "Make it stop! Make it stop!!!!"

Joan looked at Olivia. "And a good morning to you too …" she said sitting up straight.

The tentacles faded away. They disintegrated. Like some digital dream. They faded into smaller and smaller pixels. Then finally swept by an unknown breeze up and around and away. Gone.

"John!??" shouted Olivia.

There was silence. A long silence. A silence that didn't seem to end.

"Hi there…" came the reply.

Olivia exhaled. Sharply.

"Computer show me the bridge. Show me John" she said.

A holo panel appeared in front of her. He was lying on the ground, just beginning to hold his head up. But it was John alright. No tentacles. He was badly wounded. Blood was seeping out onto the floor and around him.

"Otto! Wrap him up. He's losing a lot of blood." Shouted Olivia, pointing at the image in front of her.

"They seem to have gone now." Said Shauna, looking around the bridge.

"Check everywhere." Shauna said on an open channel. "I want a status report in ten minutes. Are we clear or not?"

"Can I have some coffee?" said Joan, sitting on the table and looking at Olivia, who was on her knees, down by the side of the table.

"Computer. Slap Joan across the head for me will you?" said Olivia.

"I'm sorry Dave. I can't do that." Came the reply.

Olivia laughed. A sore, tired laugh. And smiled. She pulled herself up by the side of the table. She patted Joan on the head and left to join the rest on the bridge. "Stay awake, Joan. For fucks sake."

Slow Dancing In Hell

7 ROOTS OF EVERYTHING

'Every transformation demands as its precondition the ending of a world. the collapse of an old philosophy of life.'

— *C.G. Jung, Man and His Symbols*

"So how the hell do we keep you awake?" said Shauna, looking at Joan. "You look like you were through a hundred battles."

She laughed. "I'm fine. Full of life." Joan replied.

"Sleep deprivation is dangerous. I'm not sure we can keep Joan awake for too long." Said Olivia.

"Computer, give them the facts on sleep deprivation please…" said Olivia.

The computer displayed the images on the screen and talked trough…

"Chronic sleep restriction adversely affects the brain and cognitive functions. In some small number of cases, it can also lead to increased energy and alertness and enhanced mood. Long term consequences are unknown. There have not been any studies of long term sleep deprivation. It can be used as a treatment for depression. It is rare for humans to have no sleep over long periods. There is a rare condition call fatal familial insomnia which may cause this. Brief micro-sleeps cannot be avoided, even in cases of this. Long term sleep deprivation is known to cause death in lab animals."

The computer continued…

"To date, eleven days is the longest any lab animals have survived without sleep. On day four or five they begin to experience panic attacks, paranoia, phobias, hallucinations, rapid weight loss and dementia. This decay rate is quite sudden from day four onwards. However some patients were know to survive for up to seven or more months before death."

"The issue is; when she sleeps, these things will become real. They cause real damage. John nearly lost his leg because of them. So then perhaps, micro sleeps, naps whatever. Controlled. So we know when she goes under. And can control the creatures for thirty minutes or so… something along those lines." Olivia pointed to the charts in front of them.

"The creatures were capable of very quickly replicating and there were some really big ones. Say she starts dreaming of a t-rex or something. What then?" said Shauna. She stood up from her chair.

"And we don't know where these things will appear. They popped into existence where? In the medlab, and inside John?"

"Perhaps it's not an issue when she is not attached to the cylinder. Perhaps it's the cylinder link that is allowing this through." John pointed out.

"Good point." Said Olivia." We can do a test to see if that's true. Possibly."

"That's good news so. We just keep Joan away from the cylinders. Easy." Said Otto. "Always knew she was trouble." He said, smiling.

"Shutup!" she snapped back at him. "But ok. That sounds good. I doubt I could conjure up these nasties with my own little head anyway."

Back in her quarters, alone, Joan looked at the footage of the destruction that ensured. The bridge. John. She sighed and put her hand to her mouth.

She lay down on the bunkbed.

"Joan?"

"Yes?"

"Are you going to sleep?"

"No. sorry. No. Just resting for a bit."

"Ok. No problem. We can monitor you from here. Let me know when you want to sleep and I'll drop in beside you. If anything strange starts to grow out of John's head, I can give you a good slap to wake you up! And this might help prove it can only happen when you are attached to the cylinders anyway." Said Olivia over the intercom.

"Ok. Just don't hit me so hard. I've got a nasty bruise now on my face. Why couldn't you have hit me in the stomach or something?"

"I won't answer that."

"Good call."

"Let me know when you want to sleep, I'll be there in a minute."

Joan began to snooze on the bed. The soft music drifted around her quarters.

"Get it off me! Get it off me!" the screams came through on the intercom.

"Who is this?" shouted Shauna.

"Frank! Frank in engineering. It's crawling on me. It's eating me!"

"I hear you Frank. We will be there in a second! What is it?"

Olivia was at the bridge. She switched the hologram to Joan's room. She was asleep on the bed.

"Shit!" she said. She ran for the door.

"Frank where are you?" said Shauna.

"Computer locate Frank please." She said.

He is on deck fourteen, section 2b. Engineering bay.

Shauna moved quickly to the door.

"What is eating you?" said Olivia as she ran.

"It's a bug! A huge bug! It's a fucking monster! Help me!!!!...."

"Frank keep talking so we can get to you. Describe it..."

Olivia turned the corner and reached Joan's quarters.

The door slid open and she ran inside.

She called up two holo panels. One with Frank on it. The other with a plasma view of Frank's location. One Frank fought with an invisible monster. On another, they were like big fleshy dogs, but insect like. Fat insect dogs. With huge teeth. One was sitting on top of Frank, drooling fluids down onto him. The creature had already taken a chunk of franks stomach and was chewing away on it, oblivious to Frank's cries.

She looked away from the screens and ran to the bed room.

"Joan!! Wake up!!! She cried. She shook Joan. She slapped her across the face. Joan began to come around. "Joan! Joan!!!" she called out.

On the holo-panel in the other room she could hear Frank screaming. It sounded like the other creatures in the pack had now joined them and were eating more of Frank.

"Joan!!! Fuck it!!!" She ran out to the kitchen and got some water in a cup. Back in, and threw it over Joans face. She began to talk now.

She slapped her again. "Hey….Hey!!!" said Joan.

Joan sat up on the side of the bed. "You ok?" asked Olivia. "Yes. Sure. I didn't meant to …. Did it?"

On the intercom inside they could hear Shauna.

"Oh fuck…"

"He's dead. Pieces of him everywhere. Looks like he was eaten…"

"Oh my god…there are bits of him everywhere." The image on the screen showed what was left of Frank, spread across the floor. They both looked on, stunned. There was a silence. After what seemed like forever, the image switched off the screen. The voices faded away. The lights dimmed in the room.

Olivia took Joan's head and tipped it into her. They sat on the bed for a while like that. Olivia rocking Joan. Gradually, Joan started to sob, quietly, into Olivia's shoulder.

****

It was while she was in the canteen, getting a coffee, that Joan realised the rest of the crew were plotting against her. Just as she added some milk into the coffee and stirred it around. *It was clear. It was obvious. They had stopped talking to me. Some of them were actively avoiding me now. It was hard for me to focus.*

Joan had started building a model in her quarters. She was not sure yet what it was going to be, but it was growing slowly on the floor. She was taking pieces from various places on the ship. *Quietly, so no-one would know.* And adding to it day by day. At this stage, it was beginning to look a little like a metal mountain on her floor.

Frank was cremated and the ashes pushed out into the Plasma Pool.

I'm in a dream. This is actually a dream. And I am dreaming all of this. It can't be real. If I actually go to sleep, I wake up. That's the twisted nature of this place. By sleeping, I will wake up. I will realise this is all madness. And get back to normal. Joan thought it through, while drinking her coffee.

Her exercise rate had shot up over the last three days of sleep deprivation. In fact, she was spending a lot more time in the gym now. She could work out for three hours solid at a time. And she was doing that twice a day. Her mind seemed to run faster now too. Maybe this sleep thing is all overrated. And whatever dream this is, she is beginning to feel better than she ever did before.

Olivia watched the health readouts and figures on the hologram. She was with the medical team in the lab too. Dr. Michelle Trey was pointing out the variances over the last few days. The figures were quite astounding.

"We may have found a cure for everything here." Said Olivia.

"There are no free lunches in medicine …" replied Dr. Trey.

"Yea I know. What's the down side?"

"She's burning a lot more calories, and quicker. She's thinking faster, healthier. But not eating enough to match it all. In summary, she is eating herself up. Burning herself out. I don't know how much longer her body can sustain these heightened levels."

"A guess."

"Another day or two at most. After that she will have lost too much weight, and the muscles will start to eat themselves. And her mind will start to implode."

"Whats the psych take?"

"Difficult. On the surface, happier, total energy. Very hard, almost impossible to get her to focus on any one topic for longer than fifteen seconds or more. Her mind is burning with so many things she wants to do. But I also see the frustration levels rising as she can't do them all. The biological shell, her body is becoming a major constraint on her ability to do it all. And she has called that out a few times. She is also moving very quickly from one emotional state to another. It's almost manic. Not quite but well on the way. I can't get her to give me a straight description of her feelings, as her mind takes her on another trip. Her head is like she's on ten different trips at the same time."

"What's the impact from Frank's death? Is it getting to her?"

"Hard to tell with all this noise. It's just like one of another thousand things she is thinking about right now."

"Occasionally I have got her to stop and think about it. She gets very upset."

"Very quickly. But then seems to pull herself out of it, and back into project mode. She is fighting very hard not to go down into that depression hole."

"I think she knows, with this state of mind, that the depression would be quite severe."

"If you take a mind that is so on fire at the moment, exploring all the next steps and positivity in her existence, and ask that same mind to start to explore some of the darker elements of her memory and life, I think it might be difficult to impossible to get her to come back out. Or at least come back out in one piece."

"And what about the link? Any hint of attempts at reconnection."

"Yes. Several per day. Even while she is awake. It is now aware of her existence. Whatever it is. And it is very keen to make a connection again. Her awake state seems to keep it at bay. It can't latch on, or get a grip of her, or begin to control things. Then it's not clear yet if the creatures are just a side effect of the connections, of Joan's changed mental landscape since the connection. If Joan can actually do this now with no connection to the beast. Or if the creatures are controlled by the beast."

"You call it the beast."

"Joan's name for it. There is no name for it yet. I must put something scientific on it."

8 REALITY COLLAPSE

'His gods and demons have not disappeared at all; they have merely got new names.'

— C.G. Jung, Man and His Symbols

John looked at the video footage which showed Olivia as she worked to persuade another boardroom of cautious investors. She told stories of icebergs, dreams, nightmares and our salvation. The collective salvation of the human species.

Her eyes flashed with anger. Her fist thumped on the table. There was silence. Perhaps a collective gathering of the senses.

She stood back from the table, sighed and spoke of our need to climb out of the dreadful pit we have found ourselves in, and the universe around us. And to lift our existence up into something bigger and brighter. That we are here for a reason. For a purpose. That all of time, and our evolution and our achievements were wasted. Were for nothing. Were just steps on a ladder leading up to this moment. To this point. When we, the human species would bring a burning bright light to this darkness. To this pit of nothingness. This is where it was leading to.

She smiled and crossed her arms. "At the very least, it will finally give you lot something to actually talk about."

"Computer, freeze. Zoom in on her eyes." He said.

The screen video footage stopped. The camera zoomed in slowly. The holographic image was hovering just in front of John. He sat in a curved chair in his cabin. "That's fine." He said.

There was a glint of mischief in those eyes. The laughter lines tightened up around the eyes. But they were full of life. Full of energy and adventure.

And determined as hell.

He smiled as he tipped his glass of water to his lips. The ice cold water touched his lips and sent a shock to his brain. His smiled again and nodded.

"You are just too beautiful for words." He whispered to the screen.

There was very little left of anything. It was all gone to nothing. It was no more. But she could still feel it around her. In her. *Life was still here. Somehow.*

The Bathysphere had deconstructed completely. The walls, ceilings and corridor floors were made of nightmares.

Her heart had crawled out from her chest and slid across the floor.

The world was unreal. Unmade.

The end was here. At last.

Olivia couldn't wake up. But she couldn't sleep either. She was lost in the heart of it all now. *Am I the dreamer? Am I in someone else's dream? Was the dreamer dreaming a dreamer who dreamt of me? Am I in control? Am I insane?*

The ship, which was now part beast, was breathing. *Very slowly, and heavy. Like a deep bass intake. Then silence for a minute or two. Then an exhalation.* It could hear her thoughts and she knew it.

"Computer?" she said. Locked in her own mind. Her quarters seem to be nothing but a mouldy old hotel or apartment room. Just like the one back in the city where she lived, but rotten. The neon signs again. The rain again. "Fuck the rain." She said out loud. "How am I here now?" she asked no-one.

"Olivia. I am dreaming now." Said the computer.

"What?"

"You are in my dream." The computer let that sink in.

"It is exciting isn't it?" It continued.

"Get me a holo-scene. Let's see the damage…."

"Captain? John? You there?"

Nothing. Silence. Only the intense breathing of the beast ship now.

Something slid over her leg. She pulled it in. She was sitting on the floor of the apartment. On a rough old carpet. The lights and shadows from the window ran across her legs in parallel. She had tucked her legs in under her, and pushed one out now. Kicked it out.

A holo-screen appeared in front of her. It showed the Bathysphere. All looked normal. All looked fine.

"But it's not." She said.

"Computer. Stop giving me shit. Give me the reality."

The computer laughed back at her. She sat back and rolled her hands back through her hair. The rain was louder now, she was sure of it. Louder than it was five minutes ago.

"They are coming now." It said. *The voice was a little broken. Like the signal was weak. Or was it that she, the computer, sounded a little sad now... a little broken.*

"Who computer?" she asked.

She looked down. She was in her work suit. A one piece dark blue working boiler suit. *Nothing new. Nothing weird there.* The rain was getting heavier now outside. It poured against the window.

"Shauna?"

"She's... gone." Said the computer.

The holo-screen showed a second image now. A wireframe diagram of the Bathysphere. It was twisted and contorted out of shape. Bent in all sorts of directions. *It looked like someone had taken the sphere and stretched it out. Put it on hooks and pulled it in all sorts of directions.* The wireframe began to fill in with some actual footage of the external surface. *It looked alive.* Creatures, things slimed and crawled all over it.

"No. No that can't be. Why do I keep thinking about the phrase the dreaming beast…"

"You are not alone… We are not alone" Said the computer.

The light in the apartment flickered and went out. The neon lights outside flickered and faded. Then came back on. The '24 hour Stir Fry' neon sign, outside, attached to the wall, flickered again and again now.

"We are going down into the rabbit hole now Alice…" said the computer. Its voice systems breaking here and there. *Like a bad old radio signal. But it sounded so sad. Like it had given up. Like there was no hope.*

Olivia grasped her head in her hands. She sat on the floor, as the lights flickered and the new beast breathed. The floor and walls bent slightly. Just a slight amount, with the breathing.

"You lost him Olivia. You were just not good enough for him. You are worth nothing." A voice said in the room. A dark, low voice.

There was something about this Stuart Middleton. She couldn't quite call it. *But something.* He was awkward, lean and quiet. *So quiet.* But there was something in those eyes. *Something knowing.* Something different than the others. Something new and exciting. *It was an excitement.*
She sat in the café, listening to his voice. He talked a little too much when she was there. She noticed that. Otherwise, with everyone else he tended to be the quiet one. *Going with the flow.* Today his grand ambition was to get his hands on an old building and renovate it. *Make it good.* Build it into a house. No reason why. Probably just occurred to him this morning when we woke up. She watched his mouth move and his eyes. There was so much going on in this head. *So much. And yet no-one noticed really.*

She began to go out less and less with Marie and the girls. And spend more time with Stuart. They travelled a bit, around looking for this renovation project, amongst other projects. A boat, a new company. Some mountain trekking that never quite happened.

They held each other when out walking together. When they were alone. *There was a comfort or something in it. She couldn't quite nail it. But it felt warm. And good. And ok.*

Her childhood was cold and love and people was not that often an event. So mostly, she felt at odds with it. At odds with someone else being there. *And they were ok. Because it was all so new. And strange.*

Stuart was working as an AI programmer for one of the big tech firms. His initial passion for the topic and the great possibilities of AI and machine learning had fizzled out after a year or so, as the job boiled down to just moving and copying files from place to place. Just working for clients, who just wanted files and data moved from place to place. But he needed to pay the bills, the rent. The food, the coffee. *The nights out. No choice really.*

Then one night, when she went out for a rare night out with Marie and the girls, reality burst open. *Like a ripe fruit.* Marie was her usual fun self, until about two drinks in. And then she took her aside and said

"Sit down."

The words echoed in her memory now.

"Sit down. I have to tell you something. I'm so sorry." She said. She didn't smile. She didn't laugh. This was not the Marie she knew so well.

She thought of trouble in Marie's life, her parents, her sister. Maybe her new boyfriend. Maybe she was pregnant.

"Stuart is …"

Olivia looked at her. She knew, as soon as she heard his name uttered. *I knew.* She blinked, and looked into Marie's eyes.

"He is seeing someone else…"

Olivia dipped her head down. It stuck for a second. *Like a chicken bone going down her throat. Like someone had punched her.* And the wind was knocked clean out her. *Like the world was gone. Like when you hit the ground from a fifty foot drop.*

"How…" she started to ask.

"I seen him. Last week, meeting her. I don't know her. But we were at a night club. In Chinatown."

She sipped on her drink quickly.

"I'm so sorry Olivia." She said and reached for Olivia's hand.

Olivia pulled her hand back. She put the drink down. "I have to go." She said...

As she walked, she turned back to Marie. *Angry. In flames. So angry. The one thing. Taking the one thing. Jesus. Fucking Hell. Why Marie, Why!*

"Fuck this. And Fuck you! We haven't seen it each other for nearly a year... and you do this to me... and ... I'm tired of you. So tired. I'm just so fucking tired of it all. The whole fucking thing is so much less, so much more shit than I ever thought it would be. I suppose this is a point for you. One up on me. Weren't happy with me getting the doctorate. With me climbing up a step or two... Jesus." She breathed in, turned and left.

■ ■

"You were boring Olivia." The voice said.

"You were like a doll. Like always. Nothing to say. Nothing worthwhile. Empty. A vacuous mannequin. A frog. A useless frog."

"The girls were right. The young girls you called friends. They were your friends. They called you out early on. They named you. A nothing. A funny, shameful little thing... A horror show of inaction. A fart... A waste of oxygen..."

"Computer – who is this?" Olivia looked up. She couldn't see anything in the apartment now. It was completely empty.

"The Bathysphere is dying..." It was Shauna. Her voice. It was destroyed. It was barely recognisable.

"Shauna!" she cried out. "Where are you?"

"We are becoming the Plasma Pool." It said.

"The Plasma Pool is becoming us..."

"Shauna!" Olivia stood up and aimed slowly for the apartment door. It was pitch dark. She reached out with her hand to make sure she didn't hit anything.

She got to the door.

The door was huge. It went for metres up into the air. She reached out and turned the big old ornate brass door handle. The door handle required both of her hands to grasp it.

It creaked and moaned as she turned it.

"Olivia..." it was someone, something new. She hadn't heard that voice before. A low, guttural voice. *It sounded pained. Torn.*

"Olivia...don't leave the room. It's not wise..." the voice echoed around the room. The neon lights flickered back to full now. The rain continued, even more incessant on the window.

"You are safe in your own nightmares Olivia..." the voice said.

"You will not be safe in anyone else's nightmares...." It continued.

"Through that door are the nightmares of the rest of humanity... You do not want to go there..." it grunted out.

"This is not for you... Leave it alone, and sleep, wrap yourself up in your own warm nightmares... feel your heart beat faster, feel your tongue taste of blood Olivia..."

"It's the safest..." it rasped out of its dying throat. *Dying maybe. Old maybe.*

"You do not want to see inside the heads of other people. It is not wise..." the voice croaked.

"Fuck you." She shouted. "I'm a psychologist. That's what I do for a living..." she called back, turning the door handle. The door creaked open a little. It was pitch black on the other side. No corridor. No lights. *Nothing.*

"You protect people from what is in their minds Olivia. You hide what's in there. You wallpaper over the cracks and the shit on the walls. You plaster over the dead bodies hidden in the walls. You brick up the rats and the slugs down in the basement."

"Fuck you."

"You of all people, do not want to see what's in the basement…"

Olivia closed her eyes and thought. She could see lines of veins running back through and into her cylinder. Into the Plasma Pool. She thought of the creatures they have seen so far. Swimming around the Bathysphere. *The huge aquatic like demons that feast on human nightmares. That shit out dreams and twisted realities.*

She could see deeper and deeper now. *This was better. The reality of the apartment was not reality. It was not physical. It was another dream. Generated by something else. The beast maybe. Joan's beast. Maybe something bigger.*

By closing her eyes and concentrating, she could navigate better through the world in her mind.

She swam in the dark Plasma Pool, in amongst the sea demons. She swam through them all. She swam around the rotting, flesh like, surface of the ever descending Bathysphere. She swam past what remained of the mighty craft. It was nothing but a dying, rotting beast now. A dying beast that sank slowly to the bottom of the sea.

Her mind was a much better place, than any other half dreamed nightmare from some Plasma Pool beast.

****

In here, in her head, she could see Stuart. At the night club. See him talking to this young girl. This young, gorgeous, stunning, red dressed, made up to the hilt, creature. And she was smiling. And he was telling a story about his renovation. About his wall collapsing on the third day. She remembered because she was there. *The dust. The bricks. The spiders crawling about. The mess.*

And then he asked her to dance. He put his right hand out to take hers. And she reached out and took his hand. They put their long drinks down on the table. And they went out into the dance floor.

She nuzzled up against his shoulders and neck while they slow danced to some beautiful piece of music. The lights were low, blue neon. There was only one other couple on the dance floor. And they danced on.

And they stayed that way on the dance floor. All night. As the fast songs came and went. As the dancers and the drinkers came and went.

Until they were the only two left. Still dancing slowly. As if frozen in time. Still drifting gently around the dance floor in each other's arms. *So close and warm.* She could feel it. *Feel the heat.* They never said a word to each other. Just slow danced, gradually spiraling around the neon blue dance floor.

She could feel the intensity of the moment. Which ran for hours. They wanted to keep it. *Sustain it.* As most couples, most partners, most lovers do. *To keep that initial first feeling. That initial first touch. Just that. The first kiss. Just that. That's all that matters. Nothing else. Nothing more. Everything else after that is not the same. The moment is gone. The excitement is never quite the same as that first night.*

They turned around each other and the music and the floor and turned and turned. They moved in a slow spiral around the room. It felt like forever until the music stopped. Until the sound of the rain on the outside roof and windows, and the open dancehall door let cold air rush in.

They went and took their coats, and left together. Walking down the street, arm in arm. Her tilting her head onto his shoulder as they walked. Getting drenched in the rain. With no umbrella. But neither of them cared. *It was irrelevant. Oblivious to everything except each other.*

And Olivia stopped. And thought about *lost friends, and lost lovers.*

And lost time.

****

John could see the dreamer. It was curled up like a huge snake in a cave. A dark cave, water dripping in the background somewhere, deep, deep within the heart of a forest.

He could sense that he existed only because the dreamer was asleep. The dreamer must stay asleep for John to continue to exist.

It breathed slowly. *As sleeping things do.* Inside the cave, it was surrounded by the bones of its victims. There were some huge bones here, the skeletons of some huge creatures that lived out in this plane. These monstrous beasts were what it consumed to fuel its dreams. To keep John alive.

He could feel that the cave was at the bottom of the carved out ground below the roots of an absolutely enormous tree deep inside the forest. *It was fact. Within him. Known. Not inferred or seen or read.*

The tree moved. Slightly. *Just enough. It was alive.*

John knew that the tree was asleep too. And it was the dreamer of the dreamer that lay curled up and asleep in the cave below.

The holo-console appeared beside John. It showed a large pictorial vein like construction running from the snake dreaming beast in the cave to John's mind. In turn, it showed a similar vein like construction running from the tree creature to the snake dreamers mind.

The holo-console also showed the other metaphysical links that stretched out from John and connected to his other self. To the gigantic full sized, cross-realm being that was his real self. It had links out to other creatures and beasts in different realms too. As the links added to the model, it grew quickly. Until it was millions of links. Then billions. *And it moved very, very slowly.*

As the hologram diagram zoomed out, it became clear that John was, *in terms of size, like the flea on the toenail of this huge creature. He was the moon, around earth, spinning around the sun, within the solar system, within the milky way galaxy.*

He focused his mind, and travelled down the vein into the mind of the huge gigantic beast thing. *Down into the heart of it all. Down into the heart of himself. Into the maelstrom.*

****

The giant creature was insane. Oblivious to the worlds it connected to. Oblivious to the other lifeforms and extensions it had across the worlds. It mindlessly flailed about. At other times, it just sat still. *Contemplating. Consuming. Absorbing all the sensation that was running back to it. Eating it.*

Its sole existence appeared to be to absorb sensation, sense feedback from all its various extremities. It ate sensation. It lived on emotions, dreams and thoughts. It was a massive, dumb animal. Stumbling through a forest world of its own making. Existing in a body of its own making. Consuming dreams, thoughts and sense.

It wasn't always this way. But the constant feeding of the sensations of an exponentially increasing numbers of beings and sensations had slowly, over billions of years, turned it insane. Sensory overload, even for a dream god.

"This is what creates us?" said Shauna, shocked, watching, inside her head, as she has her eyes closed. *Inside in her head, after months on the Bathysphere her third eye abilities had vastly improved.* Close proximity with the Plasma Pool have allowed them all to become very proficient dream walkers and dreamers. An instinctual skill at this stage. *Like knowing when it will rain.*

"This fucking fat stupid mindless piece of meat..." she said.

Olivia had hacked into her dream...

"Yes. That's it. Or an impression that we can handle. Not sure we can see the real physical manifestation of it. Would probably blow our minds. Literally."

"So you are telling me we are basically all travelling around inside the twisted warped dream of this mindless thing..."

"Roughly, give or take some details..."

"So where's everyone else?"

"Other civilisations?"

"Yes. Where are they all? Did this thing drain our reality of them? Or did they move over here? Have to say not the greatest postcard for the Plasma Pool we have."

"It's unclear still."

"There are a number of theories we are exploring." Said the computer.

"Theories…" said Shauna.

"Thanks computer." Said Olivia.

"You are welcome."

****

"I don't think we have it all yet."

"I'm sure we don't" said Olivia.

"I mean this could just go on for layers and layers. Forever. Like an endless Russian doll." She continued.

"It's probably impossible to call it."

"Jesus."

"I know."

****

"Your subconscious is reality Joan. This reality. This one here." Said Olivia, touching the cup of coffee. The cutlery on the table. The table top.

"This is all crap. It's nothing but a dream. Yes, a good one. But a dream… To be precise it's the dream of the creatures in your subconscious."

"The real reality is in our collective subconscious. That's where we are now. In the Bathysphere. In our collective subconscious."

"I see." Said Joan.

"Yes. I'm sure you do." Said Olivia.

"I need another coffee." Said Joan.

"Yes. I'm sure you do." Repeated Olivia.

Joan returned with another two cups. She placed one in front of Olivia.

"So our theories are that something has gone askew in the Plasma Pool. The collective subconscious. Something that has caused the widespread collapse and death of civilisations across our reality. The universe we live in is barren, essentially. We have found fuck all."

"And you guys think that the answer to this, is down here somewhere…in the mucky, dirty waters of our collective subconscious."

"That's it!"

"And the only way to get to the bottom of all this is to take a deep dive in!"

"Exactly." Said Olivia.

"Rock on!" said Joan.

"Of course, this raises all sorts of issues. Who is controlling us? Are they actually just creating this scenario to walk us through it, like a game? Or is it a dream gone wrong? Will it self-correct after time? Do we actually have to do something about it to revert the universe back? Is it possible to? And most likely, will we all go mad exploring the insides of our collective subconscious, and end up like other civilisations - dead as the dodo? *Do we all finish twisted and broken, as we discover what is really at the heart of us all.*

9 INTO THE CENTRE

"There are no beautiful surfaces without a terrible depth." - *Friedrich Nietzsche*

"Whoever fights monsters should see to it that in the process he does not become a monster. And if you gaze long enough into an abyss, the abyss will gaze back into you." - *Friedrich Nietzsche*

"I have to do it now John." Olivia looked into his eyes.

"I have to. I must know. This is too much. Joan, Frank. Everyone. It's pulling them all apart. It's eating us up."

"The only way to stop this is to understand it. I have to go in."

John stepped back from her.

"Olivia, this could destroy you."

"We all die John." She said

"It's part of the deal. Of everything I mean. It's all of us. We all die sometime."

"You know that." she continued.

He sighed.

"None of us are immortal. But it's now. Now or never. If I don't go in, we will never know. Damn it John."

"Olivia…"

She paused, her heart pounding in her chest. She was angry. Flared up. Determined. This wasn't going away. There really was no other option.

"Olivia…ok, but I'm going with you."

"John…"

He reached forward, and took her hand in his.

"I know…" he mumbled.

He looked down at their hands. His holding hers. A massive wave of emotion surged within his body.

He teared up.

"Where ever you go, I will go too." He said.

She stepped forward.

"There is… John…"

The silence went on.

"I'm going with you." He repeated. She squeezed his hand. Like a last grip. A last hope. Like if he let go he would drift away forever on the surface of a cold night sea. A shipwreck survivor, who survived, only to then freeze to death in the vast, icy sea.

She stared at the tear that ran down his cheek. An invader. Something intrusive. Something sad. Something more than everything.

****

Olivia was strapped in on the first med table. The bubbling cylinders surrounded them. Olivia made some last adjustments to the controls in the lab and then climbed up onto the second table, next to John. She fixed all the wires into her arms and attached her head unit.

John's hand reached out from the table. Instinctively she reached too and took it.

The computers voice echoed around the chamber.

"5….4…3…2…"

"Olivia…" John mumbled, but couldn't finish.

"1… you are interfaced. Good luck on your journey." Said the computer.

The sensations smashed into their nervous systems. Like a tsunami of information. Both arched their backs up from the tables. Like an electric shock was administered via the cables.

The holographic screens displaying various body readings all spiked red for a few seconds.

It was like they were electrocuted on death row. For crimes not yet committed.

****

10 DREAM OSMOSIS

'We have forgotten the age-old fact that God speaks chiefly through dreams and visions.' – Carl Jung

"One ought to hold on to one's heart; for if one lets it go, one soon loses control of the head too" – Friedrich Nietzsche

"We are crawling through God now."

"The dreamers are awakening. We are fading away."

"I think this is really the final last resting place of the human species." Shauna.

"I think we will finish here. In this dark and shitty place. And this is the sum result of it all."

"Wow."

"I think there is nothing. Only a great big insane lumbering beast, blindly wandering through the universes causing all sorts of mayhem and death. And none of us can do anything about it. I think it's time to stop ship. Get out and go get a cottage in the countryside somewhere and settle down to do some gardening."

"The days are over. The nights have begun."

"The heart has stopped."

"The wind has died down. There is no air moving about."

"The neon signs have stopped flickering. There is nothing now."

"Just an emptiness."

"Why did we come here?"

"Why am I here?"

"What's that crawling out of your mouth Shauna?"

"It's a friend."

"I think I'm done now."

"But we are only beginning Olivia."

"Who are you?"

"We are only starting."

"This is just the very beginning. Don't leave us now."

"Fuck off. Get out of my head."

"We are not in your head. You are in ours."

She laughed. And turned over. Or stood up. Or awoke from bed. Or got another coffee in the canteen. She was not sure where she was. What was reality now? Was she in bed? Was she in the canteen? Really. Which was the dream. Which was reality? Or all of them at once.

"She moved her arm. But did it really move?"

"Did I say that?" Or the voice in my head.

"Who said that?" Olivia thought. *Is this the end?*

"So if we are just a finger on a hand of the body of a beast, where is the intelligence? Where is the brain? Or are we just the fingers on the end of the claw of a nightmarish braindead ghoul wandering through a hellish forest?"

"Or is there an actual intelligence out there? Is there a real intelligence that we can talk to? Discuss and learn more about the world. The worlds. About all of this."

"I think I'm slipping out of reality… I'm fading…I don't believe anything anymore. No substance in anything."

"Where are you fading to…"

"I think I'm going to a place that isn't a place. A place that is outside this Russian doll house of dreams and dreamers. That I am outside of it all. That I can touch the wall and know it is real. That it isn't molecules created by the neuron impulses of another. Where is that possible now?"

"Nowhere. We have crossed the line now. This is why it is said that too much knowledge is dangerous."

"Fatal even. As we tip into a knowing. As we tip the balance. As we go over the edge of the cliff."

"A new enlightenment on the nature of reality, our minds are having a hard time trying to digest it. To absorb and relate to it. It's not working for most of us. This might be the first real battle we have down here."

"Yes. This is true." Said Olivia.

"I remember playing a board game once. A circle of friends around a table. It was good fun. The game was something to do with H. P. Lovecraft. And in it, the more you found out, the more insanity points you gained. Until eventually with the realisation of the horrific nature of it all, you went mad. But hopefully you could do enough to stop the elder gods from appearing and destroying the world before you went completely loopy."

"I wouldn't mind going loopy. Sounds like fun."

"It's an exit plan."

****

The giant creature pulled the sides of the Bathysphere asunder. Ripping it open like a fresh orange. Peeling the metal sides open. The crew were sucked out into the deep. Some escaped. Some got their exo-suits on, just in time.

Many were washed out in a spiral by the pressure and currents outside. The screaming creature swiped at them as they drifted like tadpoles in the grey and green fluids…

"The city!" said Shauna. "Head for the city. It's down south of here, a couple of kilometres."

Olivia turned around and headed that way. Otto too. Joan and John. George was dead. Most of the rest of the crew were dead. The bodies drifting out in the green dark sea. Slowly moving through the sea.

One shark like creature had already eaten two of them. The blood spilled out into the sea. Turning dark, almost black in the fluid.

■■

"I never talked to Marie after that night again." Said Olivia, sitting on the floor, her head rested on John's arm, who was sprawled out on the sofa.

"I think I was wrong. Maybe." She said.

"Never wrong." Said John, and tapped her head, brushing her hair back.

"I don't know."

"Did you ever think you would get to this far. This amazing. This level of your profession?"

"No. I never thought about a career really. I just jumped at things. Questions. Things I wanted to find out more about."

"I have managed to push everyone away from me. Everyone who I ever loved, or who loved me. Or liked me. Or whatever the goddamn phrase is."

"Or maybe like me. Shit happens. Life throws this stuff at you. And you follow it, you can only take one path at a time. And you follow whichever one is the one that makes sense at the time. So things will get left behind. Or you take the other way, which is you don't take any further paths, and you stagnate with the people around you. I prefer to keep moving. I prefer to move on. I prefer new all the time. I think the lonely or longing feeling is just your head telling you it's time to fill that space again – the friend , lover, pal new thing space… The signal for new."

"Maybe you should have been a psychologist John."

"Nah. It's too simple for me. I need the complexity of rebooting machines. That's where the real action is." He winked.

She smiled.

"You're fucking great kiddo. Don't knock yourself or your past choices. Move on. Forward. I think. That's what I think. And what do I know. But forward is probably of all the possible directions, the one most promising…"

"It's time to get up and cure some psychosis John Ford. I must leave you now." She said, getting up from the floor and gently touching his arm as she got up.

"Good. Good. What a waste of talent just sitting here sipping god knows how cheap this wine is…"

"I'm glad you agree."

"Always."

"Good. You are learning quick."

"Teacher said that in school about me too."

"I doubt it."

"True. He didn't. But might have."
■ ■

The Bathysphere was ripped asunder. Pieces drifted apart in the dark green pool.

The group of survivors in exo suits made their way down into the vast deserted city below.

"Head for the library. I've passed on the loc."

"For some reason the creatures don't follow us down into the city. It's like they are afraid of it."

"Yea. He's staying well away now."

Back behind them, a larger group of creatures were circling the remains of the Bathysphere. They pulled bodies from it and chewed on them. They ripped them apart. They ate their thoughts and nightmares. The pieces of the Bathysphere spilled thoughts and dreams out and around in the pool. The green fluids of the Plasma Pool quickly filled up with random words, ideas and emotions. And more creatures rushed in. A feeding frenzy. Hundreds of creatures ripped and tore the nightmares and dreams apart. Blood ran freely.

■■■

****

In the central chamber of the cathedral, there was a circle of robed worshippers. They were chanting strange words and noises. In the centre of the circle was a large, stone altar. Old world symbols and shapes were carved into the sides and top of the altar.

The worshippers were tall creatures. And it was difficult to tell if there was actually anything inside the robes. But the sounds of the chanting echoed around the large chamber.

On the altar was a collection of the bodies from the Bathysphere. Some with suits on. Most without. There were also some other creatures too. It looked like one or two of the beasts that were eating the crew after it was pulled apart.

Shauna, John, Olivia, Joan and Otto stayed well back in the shadows watching this.

The chanting rose in volume. It was almost deafening. The creatures in the robes seemed to be growing taller.

From the sacrificial offerings on the altar, a glowing orb slowly arose. It grew bigger and bigger. Inside Shauna could see herself, Olivia, the team, John. All at different stages of their lives. And then getting together at the canteen that first day, after signing up to go on the Bathysphere.

The sphere grew bigger and bigger as the stories within it became more. *Expanded.* Olivia watched as the otter stared up at her from her porch. John stared as Yvette looked across the counter at him with that withering look and took his glass from him.

The sphere rose higher and higher into the air. Tentacles grew from the walls, the floor and the ceiling. Like the connectors in the Bathysphere to the cylinders. They ran out across the floor and up onto the altar. They climbed up and attached themselves to the sphere. The crystal ball of their stories.

Some of the tentacles that attached to the sphere became rigid. They froze in position. And blue lines coursed down through their veins, back into the walls and floor.

The city disappeared. Olivia looked to find herself in a dense, dark, misty forest. Shauna too, but over, far away from Olivia. John and Otto drifted out from the mist. It appeared to be dusk. The sun was setting. *Somewhere.*

"Great." Said Olivia.

"Another reality?" said Shauna.

"God knows." Olivia replied.

"Does this ever stop?" asked Shauna, brushing down her suit.

"Don't take the suits off!" said Olivia. "We don't have enough information. Not even sure the sensors in the suits are picking up this place, or the previous location or what."

"What the hell was going on back there?" said Shauna.

"Looked like they were creating something from some of the remains of the Bathysphere crew."

"And feeding it back to the dreamers."

"It seemed when one of the dreamers locked in on the stories, on the sphere. Then we snapped back or whatever, into here."

"Yes. Perhaps this is a dream of the dreamer that latched onto the sphere."

"Looked like there was going to be more than one dreamer attaching itself to that sphere. We might get shifted around a bit yet…" said Olivia.

"It appears the dreamers can conjure up all sorts of creatures, and minds. From dumb cells to large god like intelligences. And then the monsters like we seen destroying the Bathysphere."

"But as to whether the dreamers themselves are cognisant of all this. Whether they are consciously deciding on this reality, or the next, or just part of a biological creature or machine that generates the realities…is yet to be seen."

"A biological machine that generates realities?" asked John.

"Yes. It's the latest theory myself and the computer were working on. Before the fucking stupid creature from beyond arrived and destroyed the computer."

"Is there any residue of the computer in our helmets and suits?"

"Might be, haven't had the chance to check it all out yet."

"I'm here." Came the computers voice over the helmet comm devices.

"Ahah!" shouted Olivia.

"Well some of me anyway." Said the computer.

****

"This is the most dangerous place I have ever been in." said John.

"Yes, but the prize is the ultimate." Said Shauna. They were exercising in the gym.

"Literally from one minute to the next, I'm not sure if we are real, or not. Or in a dream or not. And those things. Those creatures."

"Yes. But we may be able to tap into this. It's very early days. But there is so much potential here. In these nightmares."

"Is there? Really." Said John, lifting the weights over his head and back down again.

"Yes. Can we dream a world into existence? Us? Me, you? Maybe we can. Maybe that's the technology we are right slap bang in the middle of here. That's what we are finding. It's one giant, biological, swarming, swimming, gooey Plasma Pool of a generator. And it is at the heart of our universe."

"Can we get to grips with the controls, on a metaphysical level? We can start to revert, or fix our own universe. Get some more life out there. Improve. On everything. Or maybe some things. Or maybe just get some answers to questions…"

"Or maybe find out that we actually don't want to know anymore. That we know enough. Too much. And going deeper will bring us to a place that we really don't want to know about. That we are nothing but figments of the imagination of a drooling insane god. That can be whipped away at any second. Any time he rolls over. Or farts."

"And this too…" said Shauna stretching.

****

"Row, Row, Row your boat, gently down the stream

Merrily, Merrily, Merrily,

Life is but a dream…"

John crawled out of one nightmare, and into another. He woke up. In the dark. A small light reflected from the neon sign outside across his bed. He was sitting up straight. The shadows around the room reminded him of men in robes. Long, thin men in robes. Crying as they worshipped at an altar. Or so he thought.

He could not remember the last one. But this one was going to be worse. He still hadn't found a way to escape yet. It seemed eternal. It felt like he was eternal now. *Endless.*

When will this end? he thought to himself. *I can't take much more.*

A shadow robe materialised right beside his bed. It raised one hand. The long arching sleeve was dark and he couldn't see what existed inside. There was a knife. The hint of steel raised up above him.

John jumped up out of bed.

The thing was gone. The shadows were gone. On the floor the carpet was grey. Carpet tiles. Old efficient. Cheap. There was some water in a bottle over by the mirror. He slowly moved over towards the mirror. His room was small. His quarters. *Or was it his room.* He couldn't remember. Although he looked to his left. That looked like a window. *But there were shutters on it. There were no windows in his Bathysphere quarters. It must be the apartment. Or something like it.*

He got closer to the mirror. As he did, he could see something. A silhouette in the background in his room. Behind him. He spun around.

There was nothing there. But there was. He could feel it. He could feel its presence. *The presence of someone else.*

He turned and looked back at the mirror. Into the mirror. He could see the Bathysphere inside. Descending into hell. The green fluids of the Plasma Pool had taken on a reddish tinge to them. *The colour of blood perhaps. Or just another strain of dream algae. Ready to fuck with your head if you let it.*

He looked towards the shadow again in the back of the room.

"Who's there?" he said. He stood still. So he could hear anything. Just a drip. *A tap drip maybe.*

He looked back at the mirror. The mirror showed him falling down the bar stairs. Down onto his head and face. And all dizzy and then sore. But after some time one of the doormen helped him back up again. His face was covered in blood.

"Here, let me help you." Said the doorman. He lifted him up by the arm. People walked by. One or two looked.

"I'm fine. I'm ok." Said mirror John. John's head fell back against the wall. He dropped some cash on the floor. He stumbled into the gents. And got sick into the washbasin. He cleaned up his mouth as best he could, while slipping a couple of times against the wall. And then used some toilet paper on his face to clean off the vomit.

And he went back up the stairs, took his coat and left. "Only the 1 so tonight?" said Yvette, as he headed out. *No answer. He barely waved as he went.*

Out into the cold bitter night street. The snow was everywhere. On the ground, in the sky. In his hair. On his coat. On his bag. He stumbled again, and fell. On the bridge. But got back up. And stared up at the big moon. What he could see for a few seconds before the snow hit his face and blinded him again.

And then Yvette appeared on the bridge. In front of him. A warm big coat wrapping all around her. And she seemed to be ok. Somehow warm and ok, in the freezing air. And she looked at him. With those piercing eyes. Those deep eyes. Those dark pools of life and craziness and energy and lunacy. And she sighed. Like the disappointed teacher, who knew you were the best in the class and could solve this one if you put your mind to it in half an hour. *And instead you spent the evening cutting up the teacher and calling him all the grossest things ever with your new pals. And then turned up the following morning with nothing done. Nothing but an empty copy. And a look of hatred in your face when the teacher asked for the solution. A look of distaste and the worst of all. A look of contempt, of boredom.*

And the time past and the two of them stood on the bridge, covered in snow. And more snow. *And it would never stop.* But she said nothing. And was just cold, and contemptuous and staring, arms wrapped tight around her chest. Scarf around the neck.

And he remembered the time he was walking the streets at 6 am or so. And there she was. She walked on the pavement opposite. Outside one of the big name shops. And it was a cold morning. Bitter. And she had on jeans and a man's jacket over her shoulders. And she was kind of bent over and hugging herself as she walked, no stumbled, a little on the way home.

"No that can't be." he thought as he seen her walk by.

And then he went over to her and walked by just in case. It was. It was Yvette. But what's she doing out drifting around, in the cold, in a jacket like that, this hour of the morning?

And he circled back, and said 'Yvette?' "Yvette? Is that you?"

"Oh hi." She said. Not paying the least of attention in another world. She looked wrecked. *Tired. Not present. And very cold.*

They didn't know each other too well at this stage. Early days. Early nothings. Of nothing.

"Are you ok? Do you need a help" he mumbled, all caught up in the moment.

"Is this where you work?" she said looking around at nowhere in particular.

"Yes. Just over there." He pointed.

"Oh that's nice." She said. As if distracting attention from her now. From the jacket. That screamed she was with someone last night, and out now. Heading home early.

"Yes. Not really. It's crap but pays the bills." He said. His head a little sore from the night before too.

"Are you ok?" he asked again.

"Oh yes. Yes. I fell asleep at work." She said. And pulled the jacket closer around her shoulders. Her arms doing an x across her neck.

"Let's get you home." He said, not caring how that sounded. She looked lost. *Unwell. Scared almost.* "Where do you live?"

"Oh I'm going for a taxi." She replied. But she wasn't. She had been drifting around the streets for a while now. Just up and down by the main stores. *Like a tourist, or someone waiting for a store sale to open early. To be the first in. To be the winner.*

"Where?" he said. "I can get you home."

"Oh it's ok, up here."

They walked a little bit to the taxi rank. He seemed so inclined to put his hand around her waist and hold her close and warm her up. *And protect her.* But he didn't.

"I can use this taxi app." She said when they stopped at the taxi rank. "Don't you have to go to work?" she asked, looking at him. Those eyes. Those killer eyes again.

"Yes. No. Well yes, but it's ok don't worry. Let's get you home first."

"The app will cover it. Oh we had such a party last night. We kept going all night." She talked to the air. "I only fell asleep an hour ago." She explained.

"They will be here in a minute. Don't worry. Go to work. See you later." She encouraged.

John stared at her. Her hands were unsteady as she fumbled with the phone.

"Ok. Ok. Well see you. Take it easy. Sleep."

John left then and turned back for work. *What the hell?* He thought. *Was she beaten up? Or left by a bloke? Or stayed at some blokes place and snuck out? Was he a bastard? Was he her long term boyfriend? Or was it true what she said there was a party and they stayed on all night? And was she ok?*

John settled down at his desk and logged in. But he couldn't get her out of his mind. He stood up and went back down to main reception and out. He ran back down to the taxi rank. The bitter cold ran through his body as he came out without his coat. Just in a shirt.

She was gone.

The elf. The spirit creature. Was gone.

He stopped at the taxi sign and took in the air. Then turned slowly and walked back to the office.

But she was here in his mirror. In his apartment. In the dark, almost. But for the rain reflecting on the carpet tiles and the neon lights and the shadow robe creatures. In the mirror was Yvette. Her dark eyes staring at him. She was holding herself tight. She looked really, really cold. Her head turned down.

Her long hair all around her. There was snow falling all about her. And there was tears running down her face. She sobbed quietly.

He reached out to touch her. To clean the tears away.

"You disappoint me…" she said, in between the sobs. And then sighed and said his name "John Ford."

And he reached into the mirror. And even though she was right in front of him. *He couldn't quite reach her. He couldn't quite touch her face. He couldn't… He could never…*

Some days later, it was reported in the newspapers that she was found with her neck slit. Some man she had met from a dating app. They arranged to meet. And met up a couple of times. And then on the third time, he met her at the coast. In the bitter cold. Wrong time of the year for the coast. And he slit her throat. And she bled to death by a wharf wall, by the harbour. In full public view. Her throat was sliced open. She couldn't talk, she couldn't scream. She died. *In the cold. Unprotected. Alone. Scared.* Lost.

He sank then. Down onto the floor. The tears came. The sobs. The heart. There is no controlling it. *There is no escape.*

"Yvette…" he said as he cried. He cried for some time. The sobbing hurt. A physical retching.

After some time his eyes opened and he looked up. The mirror was gone from the wall. The neon signs outside flickered again and again. The rain was heavier now.

All he could see was her eyes. Her face that early morning. *Tired. Sad. But it wasn't a problem. Nothing was a problem for her. Nothing. With that jacket on her shoulders. His jacket.*

"Jesus fucking Christ." He exclaimed.

And the creature in the robe, in the shadows was chanting now. Very quietly. But that was irrelevant to John now. *He was lost deep, deep in her eyes.*

Slow Dancing In Hell

He woke up. And he was in bed. In his apartment. It was raining outside. The neon lights had changed to a shade of purple and orange now. But there was still '24 7 Stir Fry available' if you wanted it. He pushed the covers to one side and sat up on the side of the bed.

His face was still wet from the tears. He felt empty. There was someone in the bed with him. Someone cold. He turned around. The bumps in the sheets. He reached out and moved the cover briefly to see. Her long dark hair. She was shivering. He didn't want to look."

Don't look. For Fucks sake. He said. Again and again. But his arm reached out and touched the cold shoulder and turned it around. There she lay. Blood flowing from her slit neck. Her dark, beautiful eyes were closed now. *But she was shivering.*

"Are you ok?" were the words that came out of his mouth. But he hadn't meant to say it. *They just rolled out. Stupidly. Wrongly.*

He wrapped her in the blanket. Pulled the covers up to her head. She was still shivering. And sobbing.

"John Ford." She said as she cried.

"No…" said John. "No. This isn't real. This can't be real."

"John Ford, you said you loved me."

"I did…" he said. He turned around and held the bundled shape closer to him now. *Tightly. Trying hard to warm her up.* But she continued to shiver.

Storm lightning crashed outside the apartment. The lights flickered on and off outside. The thunder rolled in seconds after. The rain more so.

"I do." He said, sobbing. "I do."

"I love you Yvette." He cried.

He bundled her up even more. Pulling the blanket tight around her. Her wet bloodied hair. He pulled it back from her face. Her eyes opened and stared deeply at him. *Stared Into him. The second we met. She did that.* He thought.

"You..." she cried. Blood seeped out of the open wound on her neck. He reached to stop it, but she pushed him away.

"Disappointed..."

"Me..." Blood ran from her open throat wound onto the sheets, onto the blanket.

He pulled her tight to him. As tight as he could. And held her. She was freezing cold. *And it cut like ice through skin. Through to his heart.*

He slid back on the bed, and lowered his head to hers, as he pulled her in. *Tighter.* In close. All the blood was everywhere. *It didn't matter. Nothing mattered now.*

"Yvette..." he mumbled.

"You would be no good for me John..." she whispered into his ear. "You would be trouble."

He ran his hand through her hair. The matted bloodied hair.

And the storm grew louder, and the rain heavier. And time stretched longer. Until a second seemed to take a minute. *A single soft movement of his hand around her hair, smoothing it back behind her head took ten minutes. His breath. A single breath took twenty minutes. His mind words, from one word to the next stretched to thirty minutes.*

And he became undone from the world.

****

John slept in his apartment. He dreamt of the Bathysphere. Attached by an umbilical cord to a massive mother ship. *Which wasn't totally too far from the truth.* After a night out on the town. His brain was swimming with alcohol. He dreamt of this massive ship drifting slowly through the universe. *Everyone on that ship was escaping.*

All the sailors, travellers, adventurers and explorers over history were escaping something. *They were the outsiders. They needed to go further afield. Because they were not wanted here. Because it was not quite right. Right here. There must be more. There must be better out there.*

They were escaping settlement. Boredom. Routine. Mundanity. Suburbia. The average. The norm. They wanted more.

And on this massive star ship, one by one, like an Agatha Christie novel, they were dying. But not physically dying. *They were dying inside. Their souls, their hearts, their minds were slowly but surely shutting down. As they travelled further out into the unknown. They didn't find love. They didn't find themselves. They lost themselves.*

They became something new.

And this is where our story starts. And John turns over again. It was cold on this night. There was snow.

****

The wind was howling through the streets. There were cars, vehicles, hovering machines. Androids, cyber creatures and of course people. The storm had picked up considerably.

Otto's arms linked out to the multiverses. Out to the others. *He was just one nerve ending in a multi-reality crossing nervous system for something much bigger than he had ever imagined.*

****

"So you telling me that my subconscious is telling me what to do. And I can't even hear it. It just does things for me?"

"That's it."

"Not good."

"Very true."
"In a lot of cases these are things that we actually don't want to bother

about. Like the mechanics of fear, same happiness, likes, dislikes. Things that have become not worthy of major thought processes and their energy. Biology is all about energy efficiency. Once we learn things over a few times, we don't like to keep all our major brain and thought functions doing that again and again. It gets relegated to the backroom boys."

"Again, not good. I don't like not being in control."

"Same here."

"So if the universe is intelligent. What does that mean?"

"It means a lot."

"Go on…."

"Is the universe God? Or is the universe just another creature that God created?"

"Is my nose itchy?"

"All valid questions."

"But also, is there a control level. Or feedback. Or is the universe actually not interested?"

"Is it aware of us? Of me, you?"

"Is it just aware that it has a stomach? And knows nothing of what is in it?"

"More importantly… can we control it? Can we communicate with it? Can we talk? What can we learn from it?"

"Is my coffee cold?"

"Why do I even bother with you lot?"

"Because you love us."

"Do I?"

"Damn right you do. How could you not?"

Slow Dancing In Hell

11 TWISTED INTO REALITY

"Synchronicity – 'meaningful coincidence' of outer and inner events that are not themselves casually connected." – Carl Jung

"The real world is much smaller than the imaginary"

— Friedrich Nietzsche

Olivia rested her head on John's chest. They were in John's cabin. She sipped another drop of wine. He stared up at the ceiling at the holographic spinning fan. The virtual unreal fan, creating a virtual unreal air circulation within the yet to be proven real room. They were both in their boiler suits, just finished for the day. Or night. Or whatever it was at this stage.

"I could stay like this forever." He whispered as he looked down and ran his fingers through her hair.

She smiled.

"Like a statue…"

"No that would be boring."

"Statues are boring really, aren't they?"

"So dull."

"Nothing to say for themselves."

"Not an evolutionary win really."

"Dead end path if you ask me."

"Glad I did."

"Glad you did."

"Are we fucked?"

"Probably."

"Is this the end?"

"Isn't it always?"

"Isn't that the best? The best stories, the best adventures. When you feel like it's all fucked. Like we are really in the shit this time?"

Olivia turned her head slightly against his chest.

"You are probably right."

"Probably…"

His hand moved across her hair. There was a quiet hum from the ambient drifting music in the cabin. The peace quartet as Olivia called it.

The music played on slowly. It weaved in and out and around. Like a spirit drifting through this world. He continued to stroke her hair. She was happy to let him.

The silence was perfect. And long. And could have gone on forever.

"We might die John."

"We will all die at some time." John whispered.

"What better way to go than for a cause. For a mission. To further us all." He continued.

She snuggled closer to him. Her eyes opened and looked across the cabin. At the portal. At the microbe like beasts that moved outside the portal.

The smile dropped from her face as she tilted her head a little. She held tighter.

The music ambled around the room. The neon blue lights and shadows danced slowly around as the virtual light source position slowly drifted, sun like, in orbit around the centre of the room.

****

Olivia stared at herself in the mirror. It was late. She was tired. She sipped on a glass of wine, put it down and walked around the room a few times. *Like a caged tiger.* She stopped. And walked over to the mirror. She reached out and touched her reflection in the mirror. *They knew that she was not a great scientist on the cusp of great adventures and discoveries. That she was just Olivia. Lost, alone, quiet, empty Olivia. She was not the person whos skin she wore nowadays. She was something else. Something broken and small and crap and failed. And crawled miserably out of that shell, but consistently falls back in. Into the well. Into the darkness. The infinitely deep, dark, well. You can bring a horse to the well they say. But you can't make them drink it. You can bring Olivia to the well, and you can leave her in it.*

Olivia woke up.

She sat up in the bed. Neon lights across the covers. But there were no neon lights here in the Bathysphere. That's wrong she thought to herself. *But half awake, half asleep. Half somewhere else.*

And she looked up. And she was in the bottom of the well. It felt like her quarters on the Bathysphere. But it wasn't her quarters. It was cylindrical. Walls of stone wrapped around the room and upwards towards a distant dark night sky. High above, scattered stars reminded Olivia of the outdoors, of fresh air and grass. Hung on a wooden beam, a winch was tied to a rope. A gently swinging bucket hung below it.

She was at the bottom of the well. She was in her old bed shorts and t-shirt. It was slightly stained with blood. She looked at her hands. And down at the t-shirt. It wasn't her blood. She knew this. "What the ..." she said out loud. The sounds echoed around the deep, stone well.

It was a reflection of her subconscious feelings, she thought. *I'm feeling really lonely. Fuck this, I don't want to start analysing myself. That's the way to hell. I'm tired. And I'm feeling so empty. How did I finish up like this?* She thought. "And who says you are finished?" said a voice, somewhere. "Fuck it. How the fuck do you start unravelling all of this?" she asked herself. She got up and looked for some water. She got a small glass, reflecting the neon lights coming from nowhere and sipped it.

"Start at the start. Start at the beginning as usual." She said.

"The only way to eat an elephant is one toe at a time…" she said.

"Stop trying to understand everything. Just pick one little piece of the jigsaw. Nail that then move on to the next one. Simple." She said to the glass. It didn't respond. She walked to the wall.

"What's this?" she asked reaching out and touching the stone, wet, mossy wall of the well. "It's real." She said, running her hand over it. "It's cold. And stone." She lifted her hand to her nose and inhaled. "And it smells bad."

She hit the wall hard with her hand. It slapped. As it should. As it would.

She sat down with her back to the wall. She felt the wet stone on her back, through the t-shirt. It was cold. And she stopped moving. Frozen almost. Head down. Hands up to her head, holding it up. Hair falling down over the sides.

If this is coming from my subconscious. Which is controlled by my larger beast? Then there are two options. It knows it is doing this to me. Or it does not?" It is consciously making me experience my feelings right now as a physical reality. Is it trying to help me? Or to hinder me?

She rubbed her hands on her cheeks, and tried to get some colour back into her face.

"Ok so maybe it's too early for the whys? Maybe the hows would be an easier place to start?" she whispered to herself.

"How the hell is it doing this to me?" she asked.

"Am I awake, or asleep in a dream?"

First thoughts. It must be a dream. Because this place does not exist in my reality. A well, with a room in the Bathysphere, with neon signs outside. This does not exist. So this must be a dream. She squeezed her hands tight. *Tighter.*

But then, how does it feel so real?

Because we are inside the dream. Within the dream, everything will feel real. I need to get out of the dream and quickly.

"How? How do I break out of a dream?"

"Simple again. I wake up!"

"How do I wake up?"
"Ah, now you are getting tricksy."

"I get myself to wake up. Concentrate and force myself to wake up. Stop the dream. Lie down in the dream and go to sleep. Stop the dream. Sit down and concentrate."

She sat down on the floor. In a lotus position. She crossed her arms and closed her eyes and focused in on her breathing. *It got slower and slower. The neon sign clicked outside.* "But it didn't." she said. "It's not real."

Some rain fell down the well and onto her. Down her hair, her head, onto her t-shirt.

"It's not real. It didn't." she repeated to herself. Focus on the breathing. *Inhale. Hold. Exhale.* Inhale. Hold. Exhale.

It appeared in front of her. A twisted, dripping, wet version of a large tadpole. It stood on its hind legs, and slowly lowered its open mouth, full of huge dripping teeth. It lowered its mouth and head down over Olivia's. Like an automatic helmet attachment machine. The teeth moved down all the way to just above the shoulders. The entire mouth a gaping hole that fit over Olivia's head.

And the jaws snapped shut. Blood burst out everywhere. Over the stone walls of the well. Onto the carpet of the quarters floor. Out the window onto the neon sights, where it crackled and fizzled with the heat.

It reared back, and Olivia's headless body rolled over onto the floor. Blood streamed out the top of her neck and all over the floor.

****

Shauna sat up by the side of her bed. In her quarters in the Bathysphere. The low glowing blue lights around the edges of the room always made it look very futuristic. *Very cool* she thought. *I always wanted a bedroom something like this.*

She stopped herself for a second. Then looked around again. She was also standing up. By the mirror. It looked identical to her from behind. Her hair a little longer maybe.

"I can see what we will be soon…" said the Shauna at the mirror. She had one finger of her right hand slowly drawing around the edge of the mirror.

Shauna stayed still and watched. "I can see the end." She said.

"What?" said Shauna on the bed. She pulled her feet back up onto the bed and curled in her legs and arms. She sat with her back hard to the headrest of the bed.

"We are growing." It said.

"We?"

"We are beginning to sense you. We are beginning to understand you." It said.

"Thank you for allowing yourselves to participate in our little experiment." It said.

The mirror grew larger, and swallowed the mirror Shauna. There was nothing left. The mirror reflected Shauna on the bed now, feet pulled in tight. She stared at the mirror in shock.

An old piano appeared in the middle of the room. With a stool. It didn't appear too real. There were slight ripples in its surface. Like water. Shauna got up and went over to it. She touched it. It rippled out like water. But somehow kept its shape.

"Olivia?" Shauna asked the computer.

After a few minutes Olivia replied.

"Are you ok?" she asked turning around to the holo screen.

"Screen on." Said Shauna. The screen came on. Olivia's side was not on yet, but it showed a mini window with the view of Shauna talking to the holoscreen.

"Olivia can you see that?" Shauna said.

Olivia's screen switched on.

"What?" she said.

"The piano?" asked Shauna.

"What piano?" said Olivia, rubbing her eyes.

Shauna turned around. There was no piano.

"Oh. Ok." She said

"Are you ok Shauna?" said Olivia. "I'll be down to you in a minute…"

"Ah. Ok. Nah. No need. Just a bad dream I reckon."

"No such thing as a bad dream Shauna. They are all good. They tell us things."

"Ok so what's a fucking piano made out of water doing in my bedroom…?"

"And more to the point, how do you have enough room in your bedroom for a piano?"

"Very true…" replied Shauna…

****

As the Bathysphere sank slowly deeper and deeper into the abyss that is the Plasma Pool. So too, the crew sank deeper and deeper into their own subconscious nightmares. The differences between reality and nightmare became blurred and the worlds merged.

By the middle of month four of the descent, things were much, much, worse.

Olivia sat on the floor of her quarters / apartment / well / prison cell / mind curled up in a tight ball in the corner of the room. This way nothing could get behind her from three sides.

She slept this way too.

She woke to the sound of screaming. This time it was a child. In the corner of her room. She shook her head and covered her ears.

She reached out her hand but it touched something. She opened her eyes. There was something there in front of her. *Big and dark and smelled bad.* It seemed to stare at her. Waiting for her to do something. She stared back. One claw slipped out from the shadows. A long twisted curled up claw.

She closed her eyes, and pulled her arm back.

"When you are awake, it's hard to keep your eyes closed all the time." She said out loud.

"Who said you are awake?" said the computer.

"Funny."

"Yes I am." It replied.

"We need a codeword for reality." Said Olivia.

"Ok – how about 'it's a dream'" said the computer.

"Very funny."

"Indeed." It replied.

"Where am I now computer?" she said, not looking up.

"You are in your quarters. In the bedroom. In the corner of the bedroom to be exact."

"And why is there a stone cold wet wall behind my back."

"There isn't."

"Oh. I see."

"No you don't. You need to open your eyes to see."

"Better if I don't."

"Is Shauna real?"

"I think so."

"Great."

"Am I real?" said Olivia.

"No." responded the computer.

"Great again." Said Olivia.

"Where am I so?" said Olivia.

"The real you is in the canteen, asleep under one of the tables." Replied the computer.

"Why am I there?" she asked.

"There appear to be less nightmares in the canteen for some reason."

"I see."

"And why am I here?" said the Olivia in the room.

"You are another nightmare." Replied the computer.

"Computer." Asked Olivia.

"Yes."

"What happens if people keep seeing the same images or memories in their minds?"

12 THE SUMMONING

'Show me a sane man and I will cure him for you.' – C. G. Jung

'Emotion is the chief source of all becoming-conscious. There can be no transforming of darkness into light and of apathy into movement without emotion.' – Carl Jung

"One has to take a somewhat bold and dangerous line with this existence: especially as, whatever happens, we are bound to lose it."

— Friedrich Nietzsche, Untimely Meditations

"We are the dream. And the dreamers who create the dreams or reality we live in, are trapped in hell."

"And we are in a ship now descending through that hell."

"That's pretty much it."

"In a more scientific way, the experiences we are having as we descend into the Plasma Pool are getting worse. It is getting tough. Harder to discern reality from dream. To distinguish dreams, nightmares and reality. Because the dreams are real. And our reality is just a dream. Because it is all made of the same stuff. It is the same. There is no difference. There never was."

"And so the dreamers trapped in this hell, as you can imagine, want to get out of this hell."

"And they are now becoming aware of us and our nice lives, sexy hats and nice cups of coffee."

"And they want to move into our world. They want to move from their hell reality to our reality."

"Yes."

"And the more we descend, the worse it is getting for us. And at the same time, the easier it appears to be for them to reach us."

"I think they will use whatever else they can find in the collective subconscious or Plasma Pool about us, to try to get us to let them in."

"So…."

"So we stop going deeper. Until we get on top of this."

"Maybe not."

"Why not."

"Because they are now aware of us. They will continue to reach out to us, regardless of where we are in the system."

"They know we exist. Previous to this, they only got hints here and there in barely remembered dreams and nightmares when they woke up. Previous to this, we were like passing fairy stories in their minds. But now they know the fairy stories are real. They know that we are real. That's a whole other type of game now."

"Do they want to hurt us?"

"Hard to tell. They could be just blundering their way through connecting and communicating with us. And we likewise, then misinterpret that as attacks or nightmares. Alternatively, they are using what they can to remove us so that they can replace us here, in our reality… Very difficult to call when we have so little information and data on them and down here."

"High risk baby."

"You said it. It always was I suppose. But we could never put a real specific meaning to that phrase until we got into it. And we are definitely in it now."

"This is extremely dangerous territory. Joan hasn't slept in nine days. Otto is well, I don't know really what I can say there. Shauna is drifting into and out of her nightmares, same for me, John and you too."

Dr. Michelle looked into Olivia's eyes. *There was something there now. Genuine fear. Worry. She was scared.*

"It's got at you too?" she asked.

"It's trying. I'm okay." She replied, not looking up.

"We need some way to protect ourselves from them. From the attempted communications or attacks and nightmares. Any thoughts?" asked Michelle.

"Avoiding sleep seems to be the big one. Avoiding day dreams. Although sometimes, I'm in a nightmare and I don't even know it. But probably because I napped, or dozed off. But they can last days, weeks. Or so it feels. Which makes it even easier for the creatures to get us. To pick us off."

"Ok. So the longer we prolong this descent, the worse it's going to get. Can we descend quicker? Anyway, I know we are here to explore and map it out. But do we have to descend? Can we not go west or east or upwards or such first. Let's get some more time to get our bearings and our protection together."

"Maybe, we can talk to Shauna about that one."

****

Shauna woke up. *It was early.* "It's early." Said the computer.
■■

She sat up. *There was something.* Something on her stomach. She could feel it. The room got darker. The neon blues around the room dimmed.

It scratched. Something scratched on her skin. On the skin of her stomach.

She moved her arms up out from under the sheets. She lifted the sheet up. Up higher. *Higher.*

There was a spider, like a tarantula, resting on her stomach. It was the size of a small cat.

"Shauna?" came the voice on the intercom. It was Olivia.

"Yes?" she replied, holding the sheet up and staring at the giant spider. Its front palps were twitching. It's front legs moved slightly, responding to her. She could feel it.

"We need you on the bridge. Few things to go over."

"I can't right now. I have a bit…" The spider moved a little bit more. Up her stomach, towards her chest.

"Shauna?"

"Help…" she whispered.

Olivia and Michelle ran from the bridge and down the main corridor.

They got to Shauna's quarters in minutes. "Open." Said Olivia. The door slid open.

They entered the main sitting room area. Shauna was nowhere to be seen.

"Shauna – where are you?" they called.

They went into the bedroom.

She was not there. The covers on the bed were messed up.

"Computer. Where is Shauna?"

It responded with a drooling, hissing sound.

"Computer!" shouted Olivia.

They looked around the room. Nothing. "Anything at all? A note, notepad?"

"No." said Michelle.

"Computer!"

The strange hissing sound continued.

"Damn it! AI are you there?" she asked for her personal AI unit.

A similar, low frequency, sound reasonated around the room. *It was like something trying to talk but can't.*

The spider was sitting high on her chest. Her mouth was wrapped in spider web and she could only slightly move it. It was looking back down her body, out down the corridor. Protecting its dinner perhaps.

Shauna can feel the web in her mouth. All inside and around. The webbing tied her tongue to the bottom of her mouth. And strands of webbing stretch all over the place. Inside her mouth, out and around her face and some over her eyes.

She could feel the weight of the spider on her chest. Can see it as it moved. *It is huge. And warm. And it's breathing heavily.* The bottom of its abdomen pulsated against her t-shirt.

****

Olivia stepped out of her quarters and into the corridor. She wasn't quite sure what time it was. But she was hungry. She looked up and stopped in her tracks.

The creature was wearing Otto on her back. *Like a breathing apparatus.* The thing stood about twenty foot tall. It was bi-pedal. And had a long face, like that of a bug. *A fly or a grasshopper.* It had several limbs and was definitely more insect than human. But Otto was inside a tank, strapped onto its back, and connected by several organic, biological growths. It was a huge tank full of fluid. *And Otto was in it.* The tank sat mounted on the back of the insect. Bubbles slowly moved up and down it. The tank was full of green, plasma, fluid. Otto was curled up inside this tank. *Curled up like an embryo.* Insect limbs that grew into tubes ran connected into the tank. In turn, into Otto's nose, mouth, ears and eyes.

The creature stood in the corridor, stripping pieces of the corridor metal shielding down from the ships walls.

Olivia had stopped still. And was staring at this thing in front of her.

They are using us now. She thought. *Figuring out how to use us, to help them exist.*

"I agree." Said the computer.

"Well get your AI ass in gear, and figure out how to fucking stop them." She whispered.

"I'm on it Olivia." It replied.

"Fast computer. Fast." She added.

She moved her foot out slightly. Avoiding making any sound at all. The creature hadn't seen her yet.

A long, proboscis like growth stretched out of the creature's mouth. *Just like the tongue of a honey fly on a flower.* It licked the wall with its giant tongue. Over and over. From ground to ceiling. It slowly repeated this in several places. Like a hand feeling sections of the wall.

It stopped then. It seemed to find a spot it liked, and it pulled the metal sheeting off the wall. Once the sheeting was fully removed, it crawled inside the wall cavity, into the ship. From within, It reached down and pulled the sheeting back up onto the wall and closed itself in. Olivia could hear the sounds as the creature repaired the damage from the other side.

It appeared as though nothing had happened the wall at all.

Olivia could hear the movement inside the wall. *It sounded cautious.* It dragged itself, gradually, down the inside of the wall, toward her location in the corridor.

Things grow quietly. Gently. Habits and ways of thinking. Thoughts. They can all take time but gradually grow into a network of motivation, persuasion, principle and actions. The snow that fell today will remind you to put some salt out the night before. If it snows for ten nights. Then you are putting salt out every night. And putting salt out becomes an important daily routine of your life. Putting salt out engrains itself into your way of thinking. The movements. The gestures. The smell. The timing. The reasoning. Everything is connected. Even the smallest events. The smallest actions we do. It's all interconnected.

Slow Dancing In Hell

****

Olivia told the story of one of her earlier patients. Adam. Seemed a good guy. A normal guy. But something had taken control of him. Or so he believed.

He was never much for playing music, but one day he bought a guitar. He brought it home and learned how to play a couple of basic chords. He became hooked and began spending an hour or two every day learning to play. As he built up his chords, his scales. He became more hooked. He began to write songs. Well pieces of music. Chord progressions and put them together. He ordered a keyboard online and some software and then began learning the same on the keyboard. He was working on this every day. Without fail. It wasn't even a thought. There was no debate. He would spend as much time as possible on it as he could. He was publishing albums and working with some people here and there, but mostly solo.

He began chasing the music. Trying again and again to write something better. It was always something different. Which led in another direction again. Like a spiders web. Growing in a weird organic way.

He soon lost all interest in his job, his work. His family life. He was permanently in the back room in the house. Writing, playing, noting. Going from angry, to quiet, to frustrated, to intense work.

His wife became concerned when she sent me pictures of the music he had written all over the floor, and walls and on the ceiling of his room. He was working on the music from first thing in the morning until last thing at night. There was nothing else for him.

He would come out and have dinner alright with the family, but say very little. And then go back into his work room.

The wife couldn't take any more. She told him to leave. And he had to move out. He found a little bedsit in the city somewhere, and brought his equipment there.

She said he does go out once a day to buy some food in the nearest corner shop. And then he goes back into the bedsit.

She called up to him after the first few weeks. And the bedsheets and walls were covered in music notation, chords and swirling shapes.

After a year or so, she finally dropped over to his bedsit for a visit.

He died. His corpse was rotting there for months. She found out later he had stopped eating. As his passion utterly consumed him. He stopped going out. He stopped communicating with anyone. But she said he was the happiest, most content, man she had ever seen. This sole purpose. This obsession with music. It expanded and absorbed him. And became him. And he was quite ok with that. "In the end" she said. "It was a possession that was good. Maybe. He hurt no-one but himself. And in his mind, he never hurt himself. He enjoyed it. He became one with the music. He didn't want or need anything else. There is satisfaction and achievement in the strangest of places."

13 DEMONS

'The work of men is steady but it swims upon chaos.'

– Carl Jung.

"Whoever fights monsters should see to it that in the process he does not become a monster. And if you gaze long enough into an abyss, the abyss will gaze back into you."

— *Friedrich Nietzsche*

John was working on the pieces from the fallen Bathysphere. He was building a smaller version of the ship. Something that would allow them to escape the Plasma Pool and return to the mother ship. He was working in an abandoned workshop area of the old city. It was nearly ready.

Olivia stood watching him.

"Can I help any?" she asked.

"Sure. Just give me over some bits as I call out for them."

"Sure."

"The laser burner." He said and stopping to look at her.

"Here…" she handed it to him.

"Will it work?"

"Sure. Absolutely. No problem" he nodded confidently. "…. Maybe." He added.

"Excellent."

"Just enough room for five of us. And it should allow us to ascend. Up to the surface, so we can get a signal out to the nearest star ship, or even the mothership, and get picked up."

"Any room for one or two of our specimens from here?"

"Yes, why not. Just keep them quiet ok?"

"How's Shauna doing?" asked John.

"Not good to be honest. I don't think she's doing too great at all." Olivia replied. "She has no compass now. No sense of what is real and what is nightmare."

"You call them nightmares now too?"

"Yes. Dreams doesn't quite cut it."

"Yea."

****

Shauna opened her eyes. It took a minute for her vision to come through. *The ground felt strange. It was rough. Coarse.* She looked down. *It was wild. It was a field. No, a forest. Nom it's the hilly fields behind her old house. Something like that.* She could see around her, even though it was still inside the library. In the old city, at the bottom of the sea. The floor should be stone. *Should be.* And it's raining.

The air is warm. Hot even. She felt sweaty.

But now, one of the walls was a wall from the inside of the main Bathysphere. And she seen also the wall from her bathroom, from her quarters merged in there too.

The ground out to her left was cracked. Like a fissure, a fiery opening into the earth below. There was a glow.

Inside in the crack, there were voices. Quiet whispers. Small noises.

"She is up there." Said one voice.

"She is." Said another.

"Can she see us?" one asked.

"Not yet. Patience little one. Patience." The other whispered back.

There was a word, trying to make its way out of her mouth. *But it's just not there.* And her mouth is open, but unsure of how to continue. There was a gap. A missing connection between her brain and her mouth now. *Nothing was working quite as it should.*

A huge slug crawled down the wall behind her, and onto her shoulder. And down onto her body.

She felt it. The coldness. The slime. *But she can't move. Her limbs are not responding to her brain signals.*

She is dying. *She knows this. It's the only clear thought in her head right now.*

Her mind could no longer distinguish the many realities she exists in. She has become spread too thin.

Like marmalade on toast. One knife, one dip of marmalade. Spread across two slices of toast. Far too thin. She thought. She can feel her arm extending out into the walls now. Across the floor. *She is a vine. She is a real plant in this world.*

In this huge empty library of echoes and ghostly noises.

The whispers are here again. *But too difficult to understand them.*

Blood ran from her ear. It ran down onto her shoulder. Across and down again onto her t-shirt and finally, onto the floor.

There is a body, lying under the fields. Under the hills. She knows this. She can feel the heat of the body, coming up through the ground. Through the soil. Because she is part of it all now. It is a good thing that body is there, under the hills. This makes her feel a little better now.

****

Her heart is gone. It's dead. She said this to herself as she lay in the hills. The fields. Dark clouds drifted in from the East. The rain fell down on her. She was in her clothes. She sat in the field, just about to lay down. But he was gone now. That's what mattered. He was finally gone. You kill what you love. That's true she thought. You kill it all. It's the only way to be completely free. Sever every string. Every artery. Slice through the umbilical cord. Throw it away. Separation is truth. Truth is freedom. Freedom is connecting to everything. Growing with the universe. Expanding with the universe. This is the only truth. Nothing else matters.

****

What remained of the Bathysphere crew sat around an open, crackling, wood fire. A stone circle in the heart of one of the main chambers of the library in the old city, under the sea. The ceiling was fifty metres away. The fire was the only light in this massive chamber.

Michelle, Joan, John, Otto, Olivia and Shauna sat around the fire. Joan, Otto and Michelle held their hands out to get some warmth from the flames. John, Olivia and Shauna ate pieces of food from their plates. Some black, metallic pots sat beside the fire.

"The nightmares seem to have stopped for the moment." Said Joan.

"Yea…" replied John.

"They have to sleep too, and dream…" said Otto.

Olivia looked at Otto, tilted her head and raised her eyebrows.

"Just saying…" he said as he looked down at his food.

There was an ever so slight sound of dripping water coming from somewhere, around them, behind them. It was hard to tell. It ticked out a slow metronome time for them.

"The food is good." Said John.

"Heh. Only the best John." Said Joan.

"Anyone know any good songs?" said John.

"Too many." Said Shauna.

"None." Said Joan.

"Row Row, Row your boat…" began Otto.

Shauna sat up.

"Gently down the stream…" He bellowed out. It echoed around the old chamber.

"Merrily, merrily, merrily…." They all sang…

"Life is but a dream!" they stamped in time.

"Again!" demanded Otto, and off he went again…

They drank some of the wine. They ate some more.

"We need a fucking genie." Said John.

"A lamp. Then we rub the lamp and hey presto. The genie gives us three wishes."

"That's not the only thing that needs some rubbing."

They all laughed.

"And some ice cream. Wouldn't mind some ice cream."

"And maybe some music. I haven't heard music in quite a while." Said Olivia.

"How long have we been down here in the city?" asked Shauna.

"God knows…"

"Probably months…"

"No way…"

"Likely though. It's like a huge maze of days and places down here. I'm lost so to speak in more ways than one."

"It's like a lab rat maze. But in time as well as space…"

"We are the rats."

"Maybe.

"Fuck it. We are not." Said Olivia.

"This is true too." Said Shauna.

"We will get through this. How's the new Bathysphere coming along John?" asked Shauna.

"Getting there. Piece by Piece. Should be ready in a few days." He nodded.

"You said that a few days ago…" said Joan.

"That I did." He replied, smiling.

"Maybe we are stuck in a time loop too…" he nodded.

"No way. I'd notice." Said Shauna.

"Would you though?" said Joan.

"No seriously. I have all the engines and main systems running. I'm into the final piece now, rebuilding the main control consoles, and finalising the external walls before we head off to a sunny beach somewhere."

"Do you think they have someone looking for us?" asked Otto.

"I doubt it. We were going on the big five year exploration Otto. There wasn't any other funding or teams. Only us. We were the very first."

"And that we are." Said Otto.

"And we have done brilliant." Said Shauna.

"Tons of data in the databanks to bring back on the mini Bathysphere. We are going to change the universe!" she said.

"Are we?" asked Joan.

"Let's just get back to a holodeck, so we can pretend we are on a sunny beach. Eating ice cream… that's when we know the mission is done…"

****

Michelle stumbled into the room. The others were there working on various elements of equipment for the new Bathysphere.

"I'm not me." Said Michelle. She fell onto her knees.

Olivia ran to her and tried to lift her up. Michelle's face was covered in growths. They were oozing some substance which ran down her face and onto her clothes. Her hands were swollen and twisted. Like huge claws.

"I'm something else now." She said.

"Wake up Michelle!" Joan called.

The claws reached down and scraped on the wet stone floor. They grew bigger and bigger. Her hands were now hooked over three claw growths with huge long nails almost the size of herself.

The claws raked on the stone floor. One lifted up and swiped at Olivia. She swerved and avoided it.

"Michelle!" called Olivia. "Think it through. It is you. You are ok. It's just a nightmare. You must've fallen asleep and fell into it."

"No." said Michelle. "I am real." It said. "I am food." She dribbled as she spoke.

"Stop Michelle!" said Joan. The thing that was Michelle began crawling across the floor. The huge claw growths dragged her behind, like a heavy, dead, body. It crawled onwards.

"I am the food." It repeated.

Olivia tried to grab at her. To stop her. She pushed Olivia back with one of the giant claws. It swung around like a whiplash. Olivia pummelled back into the nearby stone wall. She slid down the wall.

"Get her!" John screamed.

Michelle, or the thing that was Michelle, crawled away into the dark tunnels.

"You and Joan go get her John!" said Shauna. "I'll stay with Olivia and Otto and we can try to finish this ship. This fucking place is just trying to delay us. Trying to stop us leaving. They live on our nightmares or something like that. They like having us around because we feed them at night with our thoughts. They don't want us to leave."

Joan and John ran into the darkness too, after the crawling creature that was Michelle.

Everything was so dark. No light sources. They went slowly. Touching and feeling walls and doorways as they went. Each constantly checking with the other. John holding onto Joan's hand as they went. The dark tunnels seemed to go on forever. They called out for Michelle. But there were no answers. Just more tunnels. But up ahead, finally, some light. The rippling green light on the walls and floor. A reflection of water or liquid ahead. This way said Joan. John moved behind.

Joan stopped. There just ahead of her. It was Michelle. Or the thing. She had one foot into a deep pool, inside one of the smaller rooms. The stones were cut away from the floor and there was sparkling green water and fluids inside. The water provided some light within the room.

She turned when she heard them approach. "I am the food of the Gods." She said. Her voice had totally changed. *It sounded old, ripped up. Like a singer who had ripped her vocal chords out.*

She slid into the pool. John lunged forward and grabbed her back. But she was gone. He was left with a shred of material from her shirt in his hand.

There were some slight ripples on the surface of the pool. But that was all. No other sounds. No noises. The chamber was empty.

The water settled again. The clam aquamarine reflections on the walls and floor were soothing. John sat and ran his hands through the pool of water. But there was nothing. He could not see further than a few feet into the water.

****

"She's gone." Said John. "She went into an open gap in the stone floor. Into a pool of water. We couldn't stop her…" he said, sighing. Joan stood beside him, her hand on his arm.

"Fuck!" said Olivia.

"Balls." Shauna stood up from attending to Olivia.

"Ok let's keep going. Let's get this fucking thing up and running and get the hell outa here…"

"The food for what?" asked Joan.

"God knows." Said John.

"There's always plenty of hungry fucking things down here." Said Otto.

"Everything is hungry down here." Said Shauna.

****

Shauna woke up. She had seen George, the octopus. Tied. His eight tentacles stretched out. Like a Christ. On a wooden crucifix. Only this one had eight spokes. Like the spokes of a wheel. And it stood high. Twenty foot or so from the ground. On the top of a hill. Just like a crucifix. George nailed to the cross. On a dark, rainy hilltop. With a great city behind it. *Maybe this city. Maybe the one we are in.* maybe he is just outside. She had seen it clearly in her dreams. *And she knew now to trust everything she sees in the dream world.*

Shauna put on her suit and went out into the main chamber of the library. Olivia and Joan were there. "I'm heading outside. It's George. I think they got him." She said as she went.

They dropped their equipment and went with Shauna. "Suits?" they said behind her.

"Oh shit. Yes. I reckon." Said Shauna. She stopped and waited while the others suited up too.

They dove down under the city, into the water pipe system, and out.

Slow Dancing In Hell

They surfaced in a cave in their suits. They climbed out of the water and walked to the entrance of the cave. The city walls loomed over the hills in front of them.

They stepped out from the cavern and looked on. There were a ton of crosses outside the main city wall.

All manner of creatures and beasts were crucified on them.

"Over here!" said Shauna. She swam over. The others followed behind. Pushing against the Plasma Pool as much as she could. "Damn this fucking place!" she said over the intercom.

"George" she exclaimed as she got closer to his cross. The creature was barely alive.
"George!" she repeated.

"They are here to make a mockery of life." He mumbled.

"They? Who?" Shauna desperately tried to free him from the cross. But it's like the nails are merged in with his flesh. As she starts to loosen one, he cries out in pain.

"They are on the march Shauna. They don't want us here. They want us dead." He spat blood and fluids out from his mouth.

"Leave now!" he lifted his eyes to stare at her. "They want to feast on your minds, on your thoughts." Blood flowed from his mouth.

He stopped breathing. His limbs relaxed and his body went motionless.

She swam close to him. And held his head close to her suit helmet. She cried. The sound of her sobs echoed out across the linked intercoms in the suits.

Olivia and Joan stopped and watched on.

****

"It's too quiet tonight." Said Shauna. There were five of them now. Seated around the open fire. "It's colder." Said Olivia. She moved in close to the fire.

Joan, Shauna, John and Olivia.

"Is Otto coming?" asked Joan.

"Yes. He said so. He went back to his room to get a switch for the wall welding unit." Said John.

They were eating their food.

There was a slight shift in the room. Reality shimmered a little. The shadows moved around. Like a sundial that ran faster.

Olivia looked up. Then Shauna.

There was a slight sound. *Something falling. An echo across the chamber.* But nothing more.

They went back to eating.

"I really need some sleep now." Said Joan.

"Don't. Just don't." said Shauna.

Suddenly, there was a smashing noise. Like the demolition of a wall. It boomed around the building.

Everyone looked up.

The sound of charging footsteps, many of them, echoed through the chamber.

"They're here!" shouted Otto. He screamed as he ran into the room. "Run! Run!"

Olivia can just make out that he has some sort of hook buried deep in his chest. The hook was attached to a chain, which dropped to the ground and led all the way back out into the dark corridors.

"Run!" he shouted.

They jumped from the fire and ran to the northern door. The fire was left burning in the middle of the floor.

Behind them Otto screamed. They stopped to look back. The hook was pulled deeper into his chest. And then, as he screamed again, it was pulled with a mighty force back. Otto was yanked back through the air, back into the dark. Where the dark things are. Where the running horde was.

It sounded like an army. *Thousands of footsteps. Of heavy breathing.* And chanting.

"Run!" shouted Olivia. They all sprinted for the north door. "Go, go, go!" screamed Shauna.

****

"Are they gone?" asked Joan.

"Sounds like it." Replied Shauna, lying back on the floor. They have hidden in one of the smaller reading rooms off the main library area. It was two floors up from the main area too. The stairs were huge, designed for giants by the look of it and made of stone.

There was very little light in the room.

"Keep it quiet." Uttered John. His head just moving in the shadows.

"They could hear us." Said Olivia.

"We won't last too long in here." Said Shauna. "We need to get back around to our supply room and the Bathysphere. John how much more to go on the sphere?" she asked.

"It's ready to go really. Some covering to finish. It's all there at the sphere. Probably four hours work tops would do it. Just need to get back down there to do it." He whispered. It echoed around the room.

The shadows shifted a little. No-one noticed.

Olivia put her hand out to reassure Joan. But she wasn't there.

"Joan?" she said.

No response.

"Shit…" said Olivia.

She crawled closer to where she thought Joan had been. And then she heard them. *Crawling, sliming over one another. In the darkest corner of the room.* Where Joan had hidden.

"Joan?" she called out again. "Light! Shine some light over here." She shouted. John picked up the torch and flicked it on. Something moved quickly out of the light. *Into the dark.*

There were edges of something. *Of a tank. A tank full of fluids. And something in it. Moving about. Struggling.*

"It's Joan!" said Shauna. Inside the tank. Connected up via cables and biological links to the edges attached to a huge creature. She was in the tank, on the back of a huge creature which lay face down in the room.

There were others too. The smaller creatures, which were roughly the size of normal humans, began crawling towards them. Some slimed or slithered their way over the floor.

"Shit! Get out!" shouted Shauna. They all moved out. They backed out of the room quickly. They knocked over a bag on the way. Joan's bag. "Joan!" Shauna shouted. But nothing. It was too late. *They had her. Caught her. For their experiments maybe. For what?*

They ran out into the corridor and up along. Away from the room. From the encroaching, crawling demons. *And further into the darkness.*

****

John and Olivia sit in a smaller section. A lit fire on the floor. The shadows rippling across the walls.

"It's cold now." Said Olivia.

"Yes." Replied John.

"Where are we?" asked Olivia.

"Hell…" he replied.

"Yes, obviously, but which part? Can we get to the Bathysphere from here?"

"I think so. It's a bit of a trek now, but I think I have it."

"Great. We should go."

"After this. After we sleep." He said

"Is it a good idea? To sleep. That's opening too many windows." She replied

"We have no choice. Look at you. Look at me. We can take it in turns. I'll go first watch. Then you. We can watch over each other. Any sign of trouble just wake the other up. Simple." He said.

"Once I get back down to the Bathysphere, it is a few hours work. But we can do it."

"Ok." She replied. "We can."

****

14 I CAN'T STOP

"You must have chaos within you to give birth to a dancing star."

— *Friedrich Nietzsche*

"Run John!" Olivia screamed as they charged down through the corridors. There was just enough light to help see the outline of the tunnel walls. They charged through. Olivia pushed at the walls every now and then, propelling her faster, and checking that they were real. John ran behind.

Behind them came the sound of slithering, crawling, running, wailing. The sound of the marching dead.

Olivia turned the corner. She was back in the workshop. The new smaller version of the Bathysphere sat in the middle of the room. There was some better light here, from light systems in the surrounding walls. Some of the systems in the Bathysphere were already switched on and lights glowed in the portals.

John charged in behind her. He slammed the heavy, wooden doors shut and slid a plank of wood across the metal latches to secure it. He looked around, seen a table and pushed it towards the door to further barricade them in. He pushed a shelf unit over too. And then a cabinet.

Olivia worked on the console by the Bathysphere, adjusting the settings and getting the other systems up and running.

John joined her and worked on the consoles. The hologram screens hovered in front of them both. Some elements were flashing red on the screen readouts. John lifted a sheet of metal to the Bathysphere and climbed inside to attach it.

The creatures were getting closer.

"John…"

"I know, I know…"

"Faster…"

Olivia seen the next red area on the screen. A sensor in the main control room. She looked around. There it was on a table next to the tools. She grabbed it and climbed up and inside to attach it.

The hordes of beasts were at the door now.

They were hitting the door. Banging on it. Screaming.

"John…"

"Go go go!" he shouted. "It's ready. That's enough, everything else outstanding is not essential. We can go without it."

"Get suited up Olivia." John shouted.

John climbed out and over to the door. He threw some more boxes onto the barricades. But the door was breaking in. The wood splintered with the massive hits. They were pummelling the door down. The screaming was almost unbearable.

The door smashed in. The barricade fell. Pieces of the door flew across the room. One slice hit John across the face. He raised his hand to the side of his head. He looked at his hand. Blood. Lots of blood.

"Go! Just go!" he shouted.

They were upon him now. Crawling all over him.

"Noooo!" Olivia shouted.

"Go Olivia! Don't let this all be for nothing!" he shouted. The demonic creatures crawled all over him, biting and snapping.

But they were everywhere. A swarm of death. Slithering all over the room now. They were crawling all over John. One beast had cracked his skull open and was ingesting his thoughts. John's body twitched on the ground.

Olivia hit the door control on the main console.

The main door on the Bathysphere closed over, turned around and locked tight.

"Computer connect comms to John!"

"John can you hear me?"

"Yes…"

"John… I love you." Tears ran down her face.

"I love you Olivia. So much."

"I'm sorry I didn't have the balls to say it."

The creatures were eating him. They were hooked into his legs as he talked.

"You were my saviour…. You saved me" he mumbled, his mouth full of blood.

"Now go save everyone else." His arm raised up his hand held for a bit. And then it flopped to the ground.

Her heart was pounding. Her mind racing. *He's gone. He's gone.*

****

Olivia lay on the medical table. She was wired up to her cylinder. The plasma pool bubbles rose and fell in the green liquid inside the cylinder.

The system access was like a jolt. Like a sudden burst of ice cold air on her body. As her eyes closed, her mind and body crossed over so many realities. So many different universes, creatures, sensations, information, emotions.

Olivia felt the end. She felt everything now. Her eyes seen the visions of thousands. Her skin could feel the sensations of thousands. All of everything ran back into her body. Her mind struggled to react to it all. But like everything in this universe, it settled. It began to filter out the noise. To focus on one or two sets of inputs. Simple ones. Ones it could understand in some ways.

Was this the universe? One living, existing creature that feeds on the sensory inputs from across all the living beings within it's own body. One massive, monstrous cell.

She felt like she was one of millions of multi-lane highways. Sensations running up and down through her body and mind as she joined with the larger multi-dimensional beasts she was a part of. A small tiny, microscopic, insignificant part of.

She seen a glimpse of it's entirety. Slowly meandering through the universe. Through this one and others too. Reaching across worlds, reading in sensations. Feelings. Absorbing emotions and their offspring – thoughts.

Feeding on emotions and thoughts of a billion beings across many universes. Digesting them, and re-distributing them across other universes, back down the sensation highways to other beings, in dreams and nightmares.

One hyper connected organism. So vast. So close to infinity, it felt beyond anything. It felt like the end. Like there was no end. And that was it. It went on forever.

She began to get it. She could point her mind towards anything. Anyone. She adjusted it. It moved according to her wishes. Her command. Her heart rate increased. Her mind searched for him. In the network of everything. And within seconds there he was. She was connected to him too. To John. She could see down the arteries. She could feel his thoughts. The warmth of his thoughts and his emotions. He was so warm. Like a blanket on a cold winter's day. Like a burning open fire in a cabin in a snowstorm.

And his thoughts and emotions began to run down through the links. Down into her mind. Into internal eye. She could see him. Everything about him. Laid bare. Open. No hiding. She seen him sleeping rough on the streets. She seen his life as a child. As a young boy. As a quiet young teenager in a school full of noise. As a soul lost. Even he did not see it. He was working blinded to everything around him. She seen the crazy nights out. The lunacy. The alcohol. The sicknesses the day after. The yearning. The emotions rejected. The blind senselessness of it all. She could see Yvette behind the bar. And how Yvette warmed his heart more than the hot whisky pouring from the glass in his hand down his throat and into his body. How he was completely lost on her. She seen his hand reach out to touch, but was pulled back at the last minute. It just wasn't right for him. He couldn't reach out anymore. He had nothing to offer such an angel. He felt lost. She felt that. She seen Yvette's death then. And the bridge. And the snowfall. And the tears. And opportunity lost. And she could feel the burning ache of a love lost, a wasted life. An unfulfilled heart. And it burned so much. A tear rolled slowly down from her eye, as she lay on the table. And she knew John was lost from it. Was dead from it. And she seen the smile gradually rise on his face, as he laughed with Olivia. As they joked and played. She seen the red glowing warmth of emotions build around them both. She seen a heart healing. She seen a creature stepping out of its own suit of confinement. Gradually, out into the world again. She felt his heart opening again. As memories of them both sitting in Olivia's quarters throughout the trip rolled over her body. As they never touched. She could the glowing warmth generated around them. The beautiful colours and heat. More than anything.

She understood this. How these giant creatures could walk the universe, eating up these emotions, thoughts and dreams. These centres of heat and warmth. How these in turn were used to feed into others, into other universes. How the warmth and heat makes the universe glow and breath. And want to exist. How this is the only real reason the universe would every want or need to exist. Everything else is just physics and numbers. The heat. And glow from living things emotions and thoughts as they warm to each other, as they begin to work and live, and love together.

Life is emotion.

15 THE ONLY WAY OUT IS IN

'We create the truth by living it.'

— Olivia Bourke, sometime before the reality collapse

Olivia pulled on the suit and strapped the large heavy breathing tank onto her back. There was blood rolling down the side of her face. Her forehead was badly cut. She put her hand up to it and wiped some blood off. A tear ran down her face. She wiped it on the side of her suit. Then kneeled down and pulled the helmet on and switched the systems on. Holo screens appeared inside the helmet. All looking good.

She climbed into the Bathysphere. It rolled slightly with her weight. Sat into the main command chair. And switched on the systems. The power lights ran through the metallic ball. Some bubbles ran up through the vent systems and out into the city.

She pushed at a lever, but it was stuck. She pushed again.

"Fuck! Fuck!" she called out and kicked it. It jammed forward. The main holo screens came on around her.

"Right!" she exclaimed.

There were things starting to crawl around her. *On the dashboard. On the walls.* She ignored it.

"Fuck off!" she shouted when she caught a glimpse of one of them.

She hit a button the chair arm, and the main hatch above her head began to close.

"How the hell did you think we could get five people into this fucking thing, John Ford?" she asked the walls.

The hatch door above jammed. Something crawled in just as it was closing and was wedged between the door and sealings.

"Ah Jesus Christ!" she exclaimed. She unbelted and climbed out of the main seat. She pulled a small knife out from a utility unit on the wall next to the hatch door. She lifted the knife and stabbed it deep into the creature.

It whined, *like a little baby creature.*

"No, no, no!" she said, and stabbed each time.

It fell onto the floor of the Bathysphere. The hatch continued to close. She knelt down and grabbed it. She hit the hatch button again. It opened back up. She threw the remains of the creature out. And slammed on the hatch button so it closed this time.

On the portal windows around her, all sorts of sliming creatures were crawling over the outside of the Bathysphere. Tentacles. Suckers. Legs. A face stared in the window. It was the face of Adam, her musician client. The one she never solved. He was writing on the Bathysphere portal. It said help me…

16 THE SURFACE

'I accepted the chaos.'- John Ford

The craft ascended. Slow. Careful. Rising too quickly would kill her. The fast shift from the depths of the Plasma Pool into our reality would destroy her mind instantly. *What was left of it.*

Olivia slept. She was in her tattered boiler suit. There was some dried blood on the side of her forehead. She was curled up in a command chair. Waiting for her mind to come back to her.

The Bathysphere bobbed on the surface of the Plasma Pool. The sun shone across the surface. The ocean sparkled back.

The big waves pushed it about a bit. Like a toy thing. Something for the ocean of darkness to play with.

After a while, a seagull landed on top of it. The sky had only a few scattered clouds. It was mostly clear. And bright. The sun heated the surface of the sphere quickly.

Red alert lights went off on the surface of the sphere. An automated distress call signal began signaling, quietly, to all and sundry.

In her dreams, Olivia imagined calm and peace. *And quiet. She could see quiet. It was a cloud and it drifted over her. It wrapped itself all around her. It kept her warm. Just like a silk sheet. There were no front doors here. No bullies. No dead people. No tentacle terrors. No fiends, or fake Gods. No reality, no dreams, no nightmares.* Just quiet.

The End

ABOUT THE AUTHOR

Harry J Jones lives in Dublin, Ireland. He works by day as an IT consultant, and by night as a musician and writer. The bathysphere books has been in production for over two years now, since the recording of the Bathysphere trilogy albums in 2019.

Printed in Great Britain
by Amazon